SAILING
THROUGH LIFE

Paul Feld

SAILING
THROUGH LIFE

A novel

Paul Feld

This book was printed in the United States of America.
To order additional copies of this book, contact:
Xlibris Corporation
1-888-795-4274
www.Xlibris.com
Orders@Xlibris.com
22756

CONTENTS

DEDICATION

To the woman who helps me feel Neptune's Wind
every day—my soul mate.

ISHINA MARIE FELD

INTRODUCTION

LIFE GOALS

Why Sailing? An excellent question, so lets start there. Sailing over an ocean on a voyage (not under power, but under sail) is exactly like taking the voyage through life. The rules for successful living are also very much like those for successful sailing, so if we want to be successful on our life voyage, we would do well to adopt the skills of successful Sailors.

I use a period of my life from 8 to 18 years old, first because they are formative, second because they are difficult and third because they are instructive.

I also use a composite character I call my Captain. Based upon a real guy who I lived most of my adventures with he has also taken on many other attributes and lesson sharing examples that were the product of others or my imagination.

I freely use 'fictionalized history' as the basis for this book to be able to have a story that has a solid foundation and consistent theme to the terminal sequence. Life isn't very often that linear.

I hope you enjoy this segment of my life and are able to also draw lessons that help you achieve more and suffer less.

May you have smooth sailing, and following seas!

PROLOGUE

We are all, every one of us, starting our journey today. No matter our age, income, or station in life, we are all beginning a new journey. And that journey will be conducted and completed by design or attrition. Your choices made throughout your future voyage will be the determining factors in your success along the course of your life voyage.

The disciplines needed to travel our life voyage successfully are universal in nature and boring in the teaching. I discovered when traveling across the country sharing principals for success that no matter how well founded, or how thoroughly documented the success of these behaviors were; when they were boring, people didn't listen. And when they didn't listen, they didn't learn, and for sure they didn't apply them in their lives.

So I began to tell relevant nautical stories which were laced with humor, adventure, excitement, and success and failures. All of which reinforced the belief in the need to adopt at least some of the behaviors that lead to success and away from failure.

The success of the stories led me to name the programs after the new theme, such as "Sailing Through Selling". The sailing (as opposed to power boating) stories were used for some good reasons. First they truly are like the rules for success in life. The sea can be wonderful or dangerous, and it can shift in a very short time from one to the other and back. Second, sailing takes advantage of the natural elements available to the sailor to 'get where they want to go' (goal achievement).

One additional reason is that if I tell nautical (sea) stories I can take from my experience, which I do a lot of, or other's experiences, and even fantasy. In fact wherever a group of sailors are gathered (especially if the group is well lubricated with wine, beer, whiskey, or like beverage) there will be a continual telling of 'sea stories', each one larger in everything than the previous one. This 'one upping' of each other has led over the history of sailing to sea stories becoming an art form. One that is laced with grains of eternal truths, and none too little exaggeration. In fact a joke is told that the difference between a sea story and a fable is that a fable starts out: "Once upon a time." And a sea story starts out: "This is no s_ _ _".

This book is designed to bring to a broader population base than just business participants, the principles outlined in the 'Sailing Through' series of courses, lectures, and publications provided by the author for business people and companies. The body of work is focused on principals which are universal in nature, and which may have been presented to you in other venues and formats already. But the nautical approach to these principals and Sailing, in particular, has a very specific purpose and design.

Sailing, of all activities, attempts to take advantage of the strengths available in nature to 'get where you want to go' without the need for significant artificial intervention, such as machinery (internal combustion engines, etc.), or other elaborate technology. Those who sail know that it matters not from which direction the wind blows; you can get where you want to go with winds from ahead (opposition), behind (assistance), the left or right (buffeting). I have heard some people insist that the difficulties of their lives are so awful that they are like air coming down from directly above the sailboat, which is normally not possible. I would say that if you found that air was coming down directly on the water you are thinking about sailing on, you shouldn't go sailing.

This book is directed to people on any life journey, and at any point in that journey. You can use this book and the principals involved to take advantage of the natural elements available to you to help in both your personal and professional quests. You have all you need. If you can read this book (or understand the principals when it is read to you), then you are ready to use the principals to gain a more fulfilling and better-balanced personal and professional life. And when you do, your example will provide an inspiration for your family, friends, and associates, someone from whom they can learn and who they can aspire to emulate.

> "Greatness is not where we stand, but in what direction we are moving. We must sail sometimes with the wind and sometimes against it – but sail we must, and not drift, nor lie at anchor."
>
> Oliver Wendell Holmes

"All of us have in our veins the exact same percentage of salt in our blood that exists in the ocean, and therefore, we have salt in our blood, in our sweat, in our tears. We are tied to the ocean. And when we go back to the sea . . . we are going from whence we came."

John Fitzgerald Kennedy

CHAPTER ONE

MY CAPTAIN—
The beginning of the story

He had a sextant in his hand, and he stood over fifty yards above me on a promontory, which formed the end our dead end street. He looked for all the world like the Ancient Mariner described by Samuel Taylor Coleridge as having a sparkling eye and flowing silver beard. He was over six feet tall with silver hair everywhere, including a well-trimmed beard which formed a line from his sideburns along his jaw to end up wrapping itself around his chin and mouth like a knot holding his face together. Boat sneakers, bell-bottom trousers, a white sailor's jersey with open collar, and a yacht club cap with black brim. He would become the most important person in my life over the next ten years.

He raised the sextant to his right eye and began making adjustments. I watched in fascination for a few minutes while he alternatively looked through the eyepiece and made notes on a small pad of paper. His face was dark from the sun and his years before the mast, and had an incredible number of lines going everywhere and nowhere. Suddenly he looked down and spotted me. His eyes were the blue of the sea in the middle of a wave, and gave movement to the term turquoise. He seemed to look right through me, and I couldn't tell if he was frowning or just serious because of his mouth being lost in his beard.

I continued to stare until the fascination began to be replaced by the fear of adults an abused child possesses, and I was just about to turn away in what had become my best defense from a potential attack from an adult, when he smiled. I hadn't seen enough smiling in my short life to judge accurately, but I would have sworn that it was the best one in the world. His face positively lit up. His eyes filled with happiness and warmth, and I couldn't help notice that now his facial lines, which before had no rhyme or reason, all pointed out from his eyes like a map of happiness, and had lost their hard edge.

His gaze went from me to the crab pot I had found and was trying to repair, and his smile and all its benefits drifted into a look of seriousness. And with that change I lost interest in him, and returned to work on the crab pot I had found along the shore of the cove, which spread out in a large circle from the giant rock I was sitting on at the end of our street.

Half of the wire was missing, and I was attempting to repair it with string. I hadn't been working very long when I looked up a little, and across the flat surface of the large granite rock, which formed a place for mooring small boats, I saw the boat sneakers approaching. I looked up higher with some apprehension, and saw that he was no longer carrying the sextant. But his hands were as high as I dared look.

"Wha'cha doin', boy?"

I looked up into the sunlight now surrounding this man of the sea, giving him the aura of the moon during a solar eclipse. "Nothing, sir."

"Seems an apt description. At least nothing very well."

"Sir?"

"Looks like you haven't spent much time crabbing, boy." With that he sat down close to the pot, and pointed to some of my handiwork. "This line you're using is nice, but crabs will chop it up easily on their way out. Notice how the rest of the pot is made of wire?"

"Yes, sir. But I don't have any." I was already sensitive to the slings and barbs of a severe lack of money for things necessary, never mind nice, and was therefore somewhat defensive in my demeanor toward this adult intruder. "I can double it up, and check the pot a lot, or put it in the water only when I'm here."

"You can do that, boy." He twisted his head back and forth as he considered my project, which on reflection was probably a real mess. "Or you could let me help you." I looked up into his eyes with the suspicion of a child who was dealing with an abusive stepfather, and surprisingly found no hint of the deceit or evil I had come to associate with an adult male, just the caring eyes of an old man. "I have done some crabbing here, so I know where they hide. I also have some extra wire, a marlin spike, and even a sail-maker's palm . . . and lots of time." The last part was said sadly, ending with a long sigh.

"How much you want?" An abused street kid didn't give in that easy. "I can only give you some of the crabs I catch, no money or anything."

The Captain looked at me with an intensity that made me move physically back a little. Then he looked me over. I don't imagine I presented a very great image. Particularly the bruises I normally sported up until I was 16 years old. I think in that minute or so of observation he came to know more about me than I knew myself. "Well. I'll need to think on that. No money you say, only part of the catch?"

I drew myself up to my full height, which was actually pretty easy because I was the shortest kid in my class at that time. "That's right, only a part."

"Sounds like we would end up partners." He rose to his considerable full height.

"Partners?"

"Yeah, sort of. Like people who work together on the same job. What part of the catch do you think would be fair for me to get?"

I looked at him with intensity this time. I couldn't believe an adult was letting me determine what would be fair. "I don't know. Maybe half."

"How many in your family?"

"Six counting my parents." Here I looked down, "there will be more though . . ." then up again, "Why?"

"Well, I was just thinking that if I'm only one, and you are six, well, maybe I should get one out of every seven or so."

Was this guy nuts? I had already learned not to look a gift horse in the mouth, so I readily agreed, but I did wonder about just how smart he might be. We went to his workshop to get the wire, and worked for a couple of hours to recreate a really solid crabbing pot. I should say that he made a really great pot, and I just handed him tools, and watched, as he explained everything, even what a sail-maker's palm was used for. Every detail was outlined in wonderful nautical terms, and when my brow wrinkled in confusion, he even explained the terms. He not only repaired the broken and missing wire, he literally built a whole new pot, and even added some new lead he had for better weight to keep the pot in place. "Don't want to have to do this again soon, do we?"

We did catch some incredible crabs with that pot over the ensuing years. I scrupulously tried to pay him his one in seven, but most often he would offer it back as a gift, usually saying that I was catching too many and he just wasn't in the mood to eat crabs, and why didn't I give it to my mom with his compliments?

Only years later did I realize that he had struck the bargain solely because he sensed my pride, and that I would, even at that tender age, never have respected someone who did something for free, or been willing to accept a stranger's 'charity'. But once I had learned to respect him and accept his generosity everything else was free of charge, and in experiencing his generosity, I began to be able to trust others, and begin to be generous without thinking I was stupid or, in our vernacular of the time, a 'sucker'. I began to accept that we were friends.

In any case, normally my offer of a part of the 'profits' would be turned aside with a question of what he would do with it, or similar response. He did occasionally refer to 'his share' of our proud work, but he never accepted anything except a few crabs over the years, and only when we exchanged gifts on birthdays or Christmas would I be able to show my appreciation.

The best physical description of my captain would be the character played by Spencer Tracy in 'Captains Courageous', just thinner and taller. I don't believe he would have accepted the comparison, but he did wear a white yacht-man's cap with a black brim and gold braid, bell-bottom trousers, and a white golf shirt most of the time I knew him. He smoked a pipe, which was most often pointed down, and his face had the etched character lines of someone who had traveled the world before the mast. He was always deeply tanned from his walks and his choice of even placing his rocking chair in the sun instead of the shade. But that tan was only on the arms, head and neck. I once saw him remove a shirt, which he promptly put back on, to reveal a pale white upper body that he apparently never let get tanned.

His wife of many years had passed on a year or so before I had met him in my eighth year of life, and I guess the Captain might have been looking for a way to occupy a little extra time. Little did he know just how much time I would require over the course of our friendship.

He also had an infinite amount of patience with me. His impact on me was profound, though only consciously appreciated many years later. He became my teacher, my mentor and my friend. The skills we used to build an adventure, you can use to build a life. I hope you enjoy the journey through this book all the more for his presence, as I enjoyed becoming an adult under the watchful eye of . . . My Captain.

THE JOURNEY'S BEGINNING

Our adventure began the next spring when I was still 8 years old but getting ready to turn 9, and the Captain and I had been working together for almost a year. I had been successfully plying the shore of the cove for food for our family: blue shell crabs, clams, mussels, and flat fish are some of the things I brought home. And the occasional lobster! In return for my part in filling an otherwise sparse menu in our home, I was given the independence of roving for hours on end without needing to report in to my mom. She just came to trust that I was on the cove and that getting food took lots of time, which it did. Especially the way I did it.

I had become the consummate dreamer. I could sit for hours on end looking out over the cove and imagining myself traveling the world beyond in everything from a Pirate Ship to a Jules Verne Submarine. I would position myself on the great rock if I just wanted to watch the cove, or I could climb the 50-foot embankment to the cull-de-sac, which formed the end of our road if I wished to view the Mystic River entrance and some of the ocean beyond.

The time dreaming on the cove had the added advantage of giving me time away from the stepfather from Hell. And the more time I spent away from him, the better I felt, both physically and emotionally. Often my Capt'n would join me on the rock and regale me with his tales of the sea, and in so doing opened up a world of excitement and adventure, which was ultimately to begin the process of freeing me from the grip of fear generated by a youth spent in pain.

I had learned to call those who owned large powerboats, and had lots of money, but very little 'cents' (as in sense), stink-potters. Legend has it that this term originated when one Cornelius Vanderbilt I installed a steam engine on his large yacht, the North Star, in 1855. The quiet war between sailors and 'stink-potters' has continued unabated ever since.

One of the stink-potters, who plied the waters of the Mystic River, and beyond, had a small flat-bottomed rowboat he kept moored at the end of our street, on the cove. He used the rowboat to get out to his big powerboat, anchored out in the river itself. He would come down the hill, carrying an outboard motor and wooden oars, to the large rock on the water which served as a place to fish, repair gear, and clean catches, as well as moor small boats. After carrying his outboard motor and oars from the end of our street, all the way down the hill, he was not only tired and sweaty, but also very short-tempered. More often than not, he would arrive to find that his small boat was completely underwater. I learned a lot of words from him, which will not appear in this narrative.

The Capt'n and I had enjoyed a lot of laughs at the hand of

this guy, and one of our most enjoyable was that the stink-potter himself was actually causing the boat to sink. He would tie the boat up too tightly to its moorings at low tide, and when the high tide came in, the boat, which couldn't rise with the tide, eventually filled with water and sank.

The stink-potter would bail out the boat again and again, only to return another day to find he had a boat on the bottom. He tried several times to caulk or repaint to seal leaks, but to no avail; his practice of tying it up the way he did at low tide always left him with a boat full of water. But he did not want to listen to either the Capt'n or me when we began to offer advice on how to tie the boat, and in fact he worked harder at sinking his boat. I guess to prove that neither the Capt'n nor, especially, a kid as small as me could possibly know as much about nautical things as he did.

One morning I happened to be at the landing when he again discovered his boat full of water. After throwing his oars at the boat and exposing me to some new and very explicit language, he asked. "Hey kid, you want a boat?" And so I became the proud owner of a small flat-bottom rowboat at 8 years old.

My Captain helped me set up new moorings for the boat, which I promptly named 'Explorer'. When we put in mooring rings for my new small craft, we also 'adjusted' the moorings for the new boat the stink-potter had purchased, which, allowed now to rise with the tide, didn't sink, so he never asked for his rowboat back from me.

And I began my first journeys to explore the cove. I also began to more efficiently obtain blue shell crabs and other seafood for my mother. I no longer had to work the shoreline; I could row out and place the pot in the best places to catch crabs and other marine delicacies.

I very soon discovered, however, that the wooden oars were too big and too heavy for me. I was always exhausted before I got to enjoy any real exploration of the cove, other than working my pot. So I began to dream about making my little rowboat into a sailboat.

It wasn't long before I began to pester my Captain unmercifully about helping me turn Explorer into a sailboat. And finally, towards the end of the summer, he agreed to give it a look.

DETERMINING THE DESTINATION

He walked around the boat, looked at it from every angle, and scratched his head. "Take us a long time boy. It'll be next year afore you c'n sail 'er."

Next Year?!?! My heart sank. For a 9 year old, next year was forever away. In fact I had thought it would be done that afternoon. I asked the question kids have favored through the ages, and which drives every parent to distraction . . ."Why?" And thus began my first major lesson in 'sailing through life'.

"Ya gotta plan 'er, boy. Can't build something till you know what you'll end up with. And, more important, what it'll do for you." In that old mariner's words are the basis of successfully sailing and/or living. "If you make this into a sailboat, where do you want to go with it?"

"What do you mean?" Like for all kids, answering a question with a question was a natural way to get adults to do all the work.

"What do you think I mean?" And his smile told me that in our year together the Captain had learned how to deal with kids as well.

"I just don't want to use the oars so much. It hurts after a while, and I can't keep looking into the water and row at the same time." I didn't want to admit that the pain in my shoulders, arms and back were really the only problem.

"Is that all?"

"Yeah, I guess so."

"Hmmm. I'll bet if you put pencil to paper you can come up with more reasons than that."

"Maybe, but why?"

"Lad, this will be a big project. There will be lots more work than we did on that pot of yours, for sure. You rec'n?"

"Well, yeah. So?"

"It has been my experience that when you begin a big project the more reasons you can find for finishing it, the more likely you will press hard enough to do so." He always kept pencils and small spiral-bound notepads on his person, and he gave me one. "Let's see how many reasons to make this . . ."—and here his face twisted up and rearranged his sea-lines into a new map— " . . . thing . . . into a sailboat you can come up with."

I was very bad at writing, but also too proud to admit it, so I just looked at that pencil and pad, wishing it would disappear. "Captain, I, aah . . ."

"I understand, boy." And for the first time ever he sat in front of me, placed his hands on my shoulders, and looked straight into my eyes. "If you really want to do something big, like this." He waved his hand over the boat. "You'll have to do things you don't want to do, like to do, or know how to do. And you'll have to work hard, study well, and let others help."

"But Captain . . ." I began. "I don't know how to write so good."

"Well, now. We can fix that, and even the way you speak. But you still need to come up with the reasons." Here his voice became gentle. "Tell you what. I'll write what you say, and leave a line or two for you to copy what I write, and we can read back to each other what you come up with until each of us understands both the reasons for the sailboat, and the writing. What say you, lad?"

I would agree to anything that took that pad and pencil from me. "Yeah, Capt'n, that can work." And I began to talk. And talk, and talk. Until suddenly I noticed that the pad was getting pretty full. I really did have quite a lot of reasons, in fact pages of them. I began to wish I had not let myself go so much when the Captain uttered his next words. "OK, lad lets go over each one." And he handed me the pad. "You point to each word, I'll say it, and you repeat it until you can read what I have written. Then you can take the book home and copy everything till you can write all of your reasons from memory."

I was initially skeptical, but the old seaman made this very difficult part of my first major project of my young life so fascinating that eventually I took to it like a bird to flying. He never called those reasons 'goals', but that is exactly what they became.

I invested so much time in copying the letters, words and sentences, so I could present them to the Captain, that they became a living thing for me. In the process of studying them and reciting them, I translated them from thoughts and wants into dreams. Dreams which I could see becoming a reality. And finally they became my new needs.

And this first of many mentors in my life was cagey enough to make that year my first self-improvement program as well.

SETTING THE REQUIREMENTS

"Don't know, boy," he would start out.

"What, Capt'n," I cautiously asked; fearing some new obstacle which might mean the end of the project before it even began.

"I don't think you'll be able to haul the lines with those scrawny arms and wrists." Then he took on a more serious look. "Maybe you could get into trouble by sailing all the way to the other side of the cove, rip the sail, and not be able to row all the way back."

And something wonderful had happened. Instead of looking down as I always had, I looked up and into his eyes with a purpose of will created by my 'dream needs', and I had the answer before I even knew it. "I can practice rowing until I can row across the cove, and back, at the widest point, just to make sure of no trouble." I offered this solution completely forgetting that my first reason for turning Explorer into a sailboat was the pain of rowing with those darn wooden oars.

Thus would begin a regimen, which was to serve me throughout my life by developing strength, early on, in my upper body. I'll bet the Capt'n was smiling from ear to ear watching me work those oars hour after hour, and day after day, knowing all the time that I was doing something with a plan and a purpose, which earlier had been too much for me, mostly because I hadn't had a plan with a purpose I believed in, and as a result had 'given up' hope of ever being able to achieve.

I would row each morning and each afternoon every day for the balance of the summer and early fall until finally I could row completely across the cove at its widest point, and return without becoming exhausted. Tired and sore, yes, but not broken.

I think that goal-setting approach to large projects was one of the more enduring of my 'ancient mariner's' legacies to me. Rowing across that cove had loomed as impossible. But when I made it a part of something else that I really wanted, a goal that I would not let anything or anyone keep from me, I then learned that I could forget what I couldn't do and focus on what I could do. Once I learned what I could do, I could then measure little steps of progress. First-row to the grassy island. Then row to the second one, and so on till I made it across the cove, and back.

Some days I made really great progress, only to find my muscles had been stretched too far, and for several days I couldn't even reach previously easy targets. I learned through trial and error that the best course to ultimate success was consistent and progressive realization of steps toward my ultimate goal. Small steps made consistently are the surest way to progress, yet there is also a point where all the work and pain brings you to a level where you are easily doing what you had previously thought impossible. Quite a lesson! But there were so many more.

PLOTTING THE TRACK

Along with planning and self-improvement my Captain had another surprise in store for me. "How will you know where you are?"

"Sir?"

"Well, lad, there may be times when you are caught in the fog, and can't see to get back home. What will you do?"

"I don't know, Captain." Again fearing that the project might be ground to a halt.

"Well, lad seems others have faced the same problem. You rec'n?"

"Yes, sir."

"And maybe they wrote about how they solved it. You rec'n?"

"Yes, sir."

"I think maybe you could find answers in the library."

"Library?!? Captain, libraries are for sissies, not for sailors!" I believed that this irrefutable logic would keep me from ever having to enter one of those places. The only males who went into them came out weird.

"You think I'm a sissy, boy?"

"No, sir!" This wasn't going well. I twisted my face up trying to make a map like one of his, all the while knowing, from hours in front of a mirror, that my skin was too smooth.

"Then I guess that we can eliminate the library as the reason people are sissies." I looked sideways at him, and he continued. "Lad, I have probably spent hundreds and maybe even thousands of hours in libraries."

When kids don't know what else to say, they usually fall back on . . ."Why?"

"Lots of reasons. But most often to learn how to do something better. Or to learn how to be faster without getting hurt." He gave me his serious look. "If we are to do this project with the Explorer, I couldn't live with myself, or face your mother, if we hadn't done everything we can to keep you from getting hurt." He drew back a little, and gave me that great smile, which formed the center of his road map of happiness. "Besides, we only have a year to get everything done. So if we can learn how to do things the right way first, by studying those who made the mistakes . . . well, seems to me like we can have you sailing sooner. You rec'n?"

"I don't know, Captain. A library." I had adopted the habit of scratching my chin as if I had a beard to weave my fingers through. "Do you think they'll let me in?"

"I know they will."

And I knew I was defeated. "Well, if you say so, Capt'n." So,

I got books at the library for us to use; in fact I even got a library card from those soon to become, for me, wonderful people. I remember the first time I came back from the library with a book. I thought I had fulfilled my part of the deal. But then, the Captain said that I should read it!

"But, Captain. This is for you. Not for, aah, not for, that is, I can't, I mean. This is a book for . . . ."

"Avoiding problems, lad. And it is for avoiding problems with **your** project, boy. Not mine, **yours**. I am only supposed to help you. You rec'n?"

"Well, yeah, Captain." I was thumbing through the book and becoming more and more dismayed at the lack of pictures. "But how do I read this stuff?"

"I just said I'll help you, lad."

I looked into what were soft, almost tender blue eyes. "OK, Captain. But it sure is a lot of trouble."

"That it is, Laddie." He leaned over, took my hands into his, and looked directly into my eyes. "Listen well, lad, for this is something you should always remember. Things that are easy at the beginning, which are what most people involve themselves with, don't leave you feeling so good when you have finished them. Leave you sort of empty like.

But things that are hard at the beginning, well . . . that's another story." His sudden smile was infectious. "The difficult stuff, once tackled and mastered, leaves you feeling really good about yourself and also adds strength to this." And here he pointed to his head. "In your life, the more strength you can add to that brain of yours the better you'll enjoy yourself, and the more you'll be able to help others. What most people don't know is that everything is easy at the end, because by doing the hard stuff you've gotten better. That's why the really good stuff in life is hard at the start."

DISCOVERIES OF SELF

"Sort of like riding a bike, Lad."

With that, tears welled up in my eyes, and I began to cry. "I can't ride a bike, Capt'n."

"I thought you got one for Christmas, boy."

"Yes, sir. I did."

"Want to talk about it?"

"I don't have the bike anymore." The Captain became silent and began to go through his routine of cleaning, stuffing, packing, and lighting a pipe, which I knew he only did when he was planning on listening for a long time. "My dad (I didn't know I was adopted until I was sixteen) took me out when we had the first thaw. He showed me what I should do by riding the bike himself. Then he told me to practice till I could ride, and went back into the house, to drink beer."

I wiped the tears off my cheeks with the kerchief the Captain gave me. "The bike was too big for me. I couldn't reach the pedals when they were on the bottom. When he had finished listening to some sports and drinking lots of beer, he came back outside. He blew up when he saw that I hadn't learned to ride the bike. He yelled that I was stupid, which he always says anyway. Then he said I was uncoordinated and that he was putting the bike in the garage till the next day, when he would give it to another kid. One who could ride it."

My silence gave the Captain pause. "You believed him?"

"Yes, sir. I know that, even if he's drunk, he means what he says."

"Go ahead, lad."

"Well, I spent most of the afternoon and evening just looking at that bike. It was just beautiful. And it was everything I wanted." I summoned up the courage to look into the Captain's eyes. "And my mom said that I paid for it with all the seafood I brought home, so it was more than a gift, it was something I earned."

The Captain struck the match, one of those wooden ones you used for starting gas stoves back then. "Having seen some of your catches I would say you earned quite a few bikes, boy." I was startled. The Captain had never really complimented me before, just his 'well done' that he always used when we finished anything. And this was such a nice compliment. "What happened?" And he started to draw the flame into the bowl of the pipe.

"I took a hammer and totally destroyed the bike, sir."

The Captain turned to stare at me with a look on his face I had never seen before. At once melancholy, and yet laced with a new emotion for him, one beyond concern, which he had demonstrated a lot of, and almost all the way to fear. He held the pipe in one hand, his match in the other, and just stared at me for a long time. So long that the flame finally reached his fingers. "Ouch!" And he fanned the match out, put it into the ashtray, and turned to me. "Totally destroyed? Can you tell me why, lad?"

"Yes, sir." And here I answered more honestly than I would have thought possible for me. But I hadn't thought I would ever cry in front of my Capt'n either. "It wasn't that someone else would get the bike, I didn't care about that. I just knew that if I let that happen, it would be something that he would use against me for the rest of my life." Here I couldn't keep looking at his eyes, and looked down at the floor instead. "He has enough stuff to use against me already. I didn't want to give him any more. And I know he likes violence."

"What was his reaction?"

"Just like I thought. He laughed and said that there was some hope for me after all."

"Dear God."

"Sir?"

"Just talking to Neptune, boy. Just talking to Neptune." He would talk a lot to Neptune over the ensuing decade. Then after an interminable pause, "Come here, lad. Lets you and I start reading that there book. You rec'n?"

"Yes, sir." And with that we began an adventure, which I have continued throughout my life, and will probably never complete. To this day I enjoy libraries immensely, and have an ongoing love affair with books. The Internet—that marvel of modern technology is just a new and more sophisticated library. I don't know if it will result in young people loving books, but my hope is that it does provide information for the next generation as well as libraries did for ours.

DRAWINGS—A REAL BEGINNING

One day the Capt'n had some particularly probing questions: "Laddie, what do you know about the cove you'll sail in?" He asked.

"Not much." I had learned early on that I shouldn't overstate the status of my research, because it was always wanting. 'What do you think I should know, that I don't?" Answering a question with a question was still my favorite method to stall for time.

"How 'bout the depth?" Obviously the Captain knew that answering questions with questions countered the stall and focused attention on the issue at hand.

"Well, the cove isn't too deep, except where it goes under the bridge." I felt impressed with myself that I could give some answer, even if it was vague.

"Don't rightly have enough information about the cove to make a centerboard, do we?"

"What's a centerboard?" I asked, thinking I would get another great lesson.

"Good question. Here, read this book, and you tell me when you've finished." So much for easy learning. "While you're doing that, I'll get some charts of the cove, so we can build it right."

My studies of a centerboard began to give me an appreciation for extensive research. I still don't think you should do so much study that you don't take action; but you should do enough to know everything you can about what you are getting into, so your actions are correct from the start.

Turns out, a centerboard is necessary to keep a sailboat on course. My little flat-bottom boat would be blown left to right or anywhere else by the wind without an ability to grab into the water and use the wind to move in the direction I wanted to go. And it goes down into the water from the center of the bottom of the boat.

Without proper planning in the design of the centerboard, and how deep in the water it would go, I would either bounce off the bottom if I made it too long, or be pushed in the wrong direction by the wind if I made it too short. So my centerboard construction required lots of planning. One phase of this was measuring the depth of the cove in all areas I was to travel, and doing so at both high and low tides.

The Capt'n asked me one question, which was to result in the need for a model of the boat: "How do you mount the centerboard and not sink the boat?" This question launched a study of the hull, how all the parts fit and worked together. And some study of the interaction of elements, the air above and the water below. It also resulted in something vital for success in almost any venture, drawings.

I had completed a drawing before the research, and I found that my first attempt at drawing would have placed me in the same category as the stink potter who sank the Explorer with the changing tides. My mounting for the centerboard had to be higher than the water line of the boat, so when the water sought its natural level, it would not enter my boat's hull. So my subsequent drawings increased the height of the mounting sufficiently to keep water out of the boat. I also didn't understand that I couldn't cut the middle of the boat without affecting the keel.

How would we cut through the hull's bottom without actually destroying the keel? We would need to construct the centerboard slot in a way, which would not weaken the integrity of the boat. The math finally worked out that we would need two positions on the centerboard, one each for high and low tides.

These and lots of other variables had me investing quite a few hours doing calculations with the Capt'n about how sailing would effect the centers of gravity and buoyancy. Basically you are OK if the center of buoyancy is above or alongside the center of gravity. You get into trouble when the center of gravity begins to get higher than the center of buoyancy. In fact I was later to learn some hard lessons about keeping those two centers in their proper place.

The drawing of plans; either in pictures, numbers, words, or some combination thereof. Then verifying your plan's correctness. These skills have spilled over from my early small boat building into so many other areas of my life, including house building, business building, and retirement planning, that I have come to believe that this is one of the most vital skills you can acquire for helping to realize your fullest potential, most efficiently. I like luck, and will always accept gratefully any and all the good luck I can get, but I think planning, and getting plans down on paper, will always improve your luck.

In any case, through our research and planning, the Captain and I discovered that I would be able to sail on over 85% of the Cove, and where I couldn't sail I could walk. On and on the study went throughout that winter. And all of the things I learned have had an application to living life well ever since.

One day, as spring approached, I noticed a new bike in the yard of the Captain's house, a blue Schwinn, just like the one I had owned for one day, months before.

"Got this bike for you to go to the library with. You're taking so long we'll fall behind schedule for a late spring launch."

I looked longingly at that bike. "But, Capt'n. I can't ride that bike. It's is just as big as the one I had before."

"Yes, but you are a little taller. And look at the pedals."

I looked to see that he had crafted and attached wooden blocks on them. "There's some blocks on 'em."

"Yep. And what do you think they do?"

"I don't know."

"Well, think a minute. Take your time, and think what they do. It's on a kick stand, so sit on it while you think."

It didn't take me long to figure it out. "They bring the pedals up." I pushed one foot down as far as it would go. "And I can reach them when they are on the bottom."

"Well, if you can reach, you can ride. You rec'n?"

"Yes, sir!" I flipped up the kickstand, and began riding the bike around the road. When I had sufficiently proved to myself that I was proficient, I went back to the Captain. "How do I work this out?" Fearing that he would make me confront the stepfather from Hell.

"We'll keep it here for now. Later, it will just seem like something you have, and your dad won't object. Maybe after the blocks are gone, you can just start keeping it at your house." He looked me up and down. "Seems to do you right proud, boy. But mind you, practice here before you go out on the big road to the library."

"I will, sir." I looked at this old man of the sea with a new mixture of feelings. "And, sir. Thank you."

"Think nothing of it, lad. You really have earned it." He came closer and put his hand on my shoulder. "Just please don't think that destroying this, or anything else, is right, or smart."

"I never said that I thought my father was smart about violence, sir. Just that it is a fact that he likes it, and I need to work him to survive." The Captain smiled and the pain that had resided recently in his eyes was gone.

BONUS BENEFITS

The Captain even had me plan a budget, which I thought particularly dumb. But, when finished, the budget made me realize that I couldn't afford to buy true sails, or a mast. This resulted in my becoming creative in acquiring the required items for the project. I first converted my mother's sheet supply into sails for the boat.

Because I knew the need early on, I was able to acquire the sheets gradually over the winter. Although there were questions from my mom about why she couldn't find enough sheets, and had to get more, they were the kidding kind of questions that gave away the fact that she knew something was up, and she thought it was OK. In addition to the seafood I was providing for the family, I was required to give half of what money I earned to mom, so I figured I had paid for the sheets, and I only took the oldest and rattiest ones anyway.

The planning process, which I had initially dreaded, gave me a new perspective on everything. Once I realized there would be ongoing expenses, I took on a newspaper route, and became involved early on with what I would come to enjoy the most about business: new ventures.

NECESSITY—THE GREAT MOTIVATOR

Back then you had to buy a newspaper route. If another boy had built it up, he expected to get paid for the size of it, and the potential income. Not having any money I couldn't do that, and none of the people I talked with would take some of my catch instead of money for payment. I did discover that the most popular paper routes were in the afternoon. As a result, The New London Day, The Stonington, and all the other afternoon papers, were fully booked. But there was a morning paper, The Norwich Bulletin, as well. And because it was an early morning paper, which needed to be delivered before school, there wasn't anyone delivering it. So, I called the newspaper directly.

I was about to ask how much it would cost me to start up a delivery route in West Mystic and part of Noank, but instead asked how I could get started, and discovered that I not only didn't have to pay for the route, but I would get free papers . . . free papers any time I wanted to entice new readers, plastic covers to keep the papers dry on rainy days, and a bonus beyond commissions when the route did better than their projections for the area, which were very low.

Incredible! The newspaper was going to help me earn money! I built that route up to over a hundred customers within a few months. Turns out people really do like to get a morning paper. And the reason there were not any morning routes had more to do with the laziness of the young people than the lack of interest in the newspaper itself.

Then I discovered what all small business people soon discover. Building a business from nothing is exciting hard work. Keeping the business going is boring hard work. I reached a point where I had to be on the road at four in the morning to be able to deliver all the papers before the school bus arrived. Yes, I was earning good money, but I was paying dearly for it. Then one day a kid from the neighborhood, Beck, asked me how it was going, and I became a businessman at nine years old.

Beck couldn't buy the route, but we worked out an arrangement, with the guidance of my Captain, where he could work part of the route for half the profits on what he did. I could sleep till four in the morning! And I was still earning some income from the part I had given up. I expanded again, got another 'partner' in the new part of the route, and finally I even sold off the original part of the route as well.

Soon I was only making sure that the papers were delivered, instead of delivering them myself. And recruiting new customers, which most of the guys didn't want to do anyway. They just wanted to deliver and not meet or deal with people. So I handled all the money, as well.

Surprisingly I didn't like the money part of it, and delegated that to one of my sisters who did. But I thoroughly enjoyed the people, and the process of selling, which to me was establishing relationships. And the relationships were almost always positive as well as productive. Basically, I learned that I like people, and I discovered early on that if you like them, and you act out those feelings, generally they return to you what you give them.

LESSONS FOR LIFE

A major discovery for me was that I didn't need instant gratification. In fact, replacing instant gratification with long-term satisfaction (which I have done so well I still don't like instant potatoes) always provides more emotional, physical, and financial rewards. Understanding that, coupled with carefully planning for your goals, guarantees your results will be better, and the satisfaction derived from them will be more fulfilling. This is true of life building, perhaps even more so than shipbuilding.

The more carefully you think through what you want your

life voyage to be, the more you will be able to plan on what is needed to 'make it happen'. Will a college degree be required? How much income? Do you need to relocate to an area where access to better education and more expertise is available? The more questions asked and answered now, before you start your journey, the better your chances of success.

Another lesson to flow from my early exposure to building that little boat was that if you do engage in such thorough planning and self-improvement, you had better plan on being the 'odd one out'. When I would want to go work with my ancient mariner, or worse, to the library, I was taunted and ridiculed by the kids who wanted to 'play'. I never have understood why others will not leave those who want to achieve something for themselves alone or, more important, support the process. More often there is not only no support, but attacks against the project and you for undertaking it. And often family and friends can be the most hurtful, well meaning they might be. So it's important to be determined enough to persist, despite the lack of support from others.

One thing my mentoring captain never said, or in any other way implied or expressed, was that anything was impossible for us to achieve. He often would indicate that something would take lots of planning, thought, work, research, or commitment, but all was done with an eye to achieving our aims. No problem was unsolvable. No obstacle was insurmountable. We might have to go over, under, around, or through; but achieving anything we set out to do was always the theme of our discussions, plans, and efforts.

For that I will always be grateful. If I had not been shown that approach to life early on, I would only have had the view of an alcoholic stepfather who believed suppression and control were how you developed young people. And my life would have been very different.

Imagine a 9 year old going to the library and asking for books on navigation, knot tying, sailboat construction, and others with the same theme and complexity. My mentor never said that I probably was too young to read these books or make the drawings; he just helped me until I could do something on my own. And he had the patience to stand there, while I struggled with words, or knots, or sawing, painting, whatever . . . and all the time I was developing the mental and physical muscle, and the kinesthesia to bring them together. This I would continue doing until it became habitual throughout my life.

That is why I have always appreciated mentors. I just don't believe that there are any 'self-made' people.

Others bore you, nurtured you, taught you, shaped you, and continued to influence you in many ways as you grew. Some supported or inspired you. Some shared in your risks, or otherwise participated in your life's journey. So we're all, each and every one of us, the result of an extensive 'team effort', and we shouldn't feel that we have to do anything totally on our own. Finding a good mentor is a way of acknowledging our need for help and making use of available resources. When all this common effort results in you're leading the team, great. But in the words of Will Rogers: "Don't believe your press." Remember that you are the result of others' efforts, as well as your own.

These lessons in planning and self-improvement have consistently been reinforced and used throughout my life. The US Navy, in its infinite wisdom, assigns crews to a ship or submarine throughout its construction. I was fortunate to be on two such crews for nuclear submarines. And I was awestruck at the tremendous amount of planning which went into a nuclear submarine. I am often told that with hundreds and even thousands of people involved, planning a nuclear submarine is different and more complicated than planning a life journey.

I disagree. Life is more complicated, and the vessel for life's journey needs, therefore, even more serious planning and preparation. The problem is that, unlike a nuclear submarine, which is so obviously complicated, life seems relatively easy, at least on the surface. One way to understand what I mean is to know that the two submarines, which I helped bring into being, are now on the scrap heap of history. They no longer serve a need. The cold war's end changed the planet and they couldn't adapt.

But I am still here, changing and adjusting with the new realities. In fact, I am working behind what used to be the 'Iron Curtain', helping people who used to be my 'targets' build new businesses and develop a democratically based market economy.

In my life, as in yours, there are many ventures to which these principles of planning and preparation can be applied. It might be building a home, furthering your education, changing careers, or any of many, many other endeavors. In every case, the important steps are beginning the venture with determination, asking the right questions, doing extensive research, developing the skills you require, and finding the help you need. This process, once applied, can be not only enjoyable, but also actually exciting.

CONSTRUCTION

In all ventures, though, the planning must lead to action. The first cut in the hull must be made. The parts made and assembled. And construction must be begun. I must admit that when the Capt'n finally said one day that I would have to make the first cut in the hull for the centerboard mounting, I was floored.

The young man who earlier wanted nothing more than to get the 'stuff' done and start sailing, was now suffering from so much planning and research that he wondered aloud, "Are you sure we have planned it enough, Capt'n?"

"Aye, mate. It's time to build."

"But what if I made a mistake?"

"We'll find out."

"But how?"

"By building 'er, boy. Now cut that hole along that line."

"I don't know, Capt'n."

"I do. Now cut."

"If it's wrong I can lose the boat." I was really full of fear now.

"What? What did you say?"

I looked up. "That we could lose the boat."

"Well, now, I guess we'll just have to consider that." With that he sat down on the chair next to the boat, and began his ritualistic lighting of the pipe. "Mind if I ask you some questions?"

"No, sir." In fact I was glad that we were talking again, and not making that hole in my boat.

"If we cut it and it's wrong, would we really lose the boat? Don't answer too quick, think on it."

"Yes, sir." I looked at that boat, and the parts and pieces all spread around the Captain's garage workshop, and tried desperately to find a reason not to begin. I just couldn't believe that we were really ready to begin construction. "Well, we're not cutting into the keel, so anything we do wrong can be repaired, I guess."

"OK, I agree. Now, what if we keep on planning, and studying, and researching, and don't make that first cut till next year, or five years from now? Then what?"

"Well, I won't get my sailboat, I guess." Suddenly, I couldn't figure out where my hesitation came from. "What's the matter with me? We're ready, and I'm acting like a baby."

"Lad, I think you just discovered one reason why 'normal' people lead normal lives and not extraordinary, or exciting ones. They never make the first cut." The Captain was smiling so wide it looked like his teeth were cutting his beard in half. "What most people never learn is that all the planning in the world is ever only the first step of the process, and you can never get all the information possible before you decide to make the cut. But the top people, the ones who do end up sailing the seas. They are the ones who realize you must at some point do what maybe feels uncomfortable in order to begin. That first cut you are facing. Well, boy, that is only the first of many uncomfortable things you will need to do, and compromise waits at every turn and every decision. But compromise is only good for diplomacy and politics." He spat out the words as if something with a bad taste had entered his mouth. "Neptune will keep you out of those occupations if he likes you."

So, we made the cut. And we made lots more. And we sawed, hammered, joined, sanded, glued, cleaned, and sanded again. Then we sealed the wood, sanded, sealed again, painted until my arms ached, and worked on that little boat every day till we had it looking like a sailboat. Well, at least it did to me.

My Captain had proved to be incredibly resourceful. One day I arrived to find a large round pole mounted on two sawhorses. "What's that, Captain?"

"Your mast, boy. You will need a mast, won't you?"

"Yes, sir. But in our budget we figured I couldn't buy it for two more months with my newspaper earnings." I rubbed my hands along the beautifully smooth white birch mast. "Captain, this is already finished. It looks ready for the boat, and that wasn't planned in the budget. Remember, we decided we would have to do the work ourselves because I wouldn't earn enough money."

"Well, the budget did call for that, but a friend helped me. So, yes, ready she is, lad." He put down his tool, and looked at me with what I called a 15 smile, as I had begun to appreciate percentages. If I ever got one of his 100 smiles, I thought I would pass out, or die from exhaustion, as I never had gotten over a 50 smile yet. "I'm impressed, boy. How did you know it was already prepared?"

"It's already stepped, Captain." I pointed to the area with my right hand, and rubbed the smooth surface with my left. "It even has cleat mountings for the main sail halyard, and slots for the spreader for the shrouds. And the top has mountings for the shrouds, and the head and back-stays." I touched a mounting bracket on what would become the top of the mast. "Is this where we'll put the pad eye for the main halyard down-haul?"

The Captain sat down and drew on his pipe, and then exhaled one of his great smoke rings into the air. Then he looked at me and for the first time ever I watched him pass a 50 smile. I don't recall if he went all the way to 100 then, but there were lots of max smiles during the following decade we worked together.

"What's 'smatter, Captain?" I finally asked.

"Nothin', boy. I just want to remember this." He kept looking, not really staring, just looking at me. Until he finally stood up, put his hand on my shoulder and really smiled once more. "Neptune has just smiled, lad. Neptune has just smiled." He paused and smiled even bigger, passing the 100-smile range I had imagined as max. "The best thing is that you don't even know what you just did. It's become natural."

And he was right, of course. I was still waiting for the answer to my question, and he was basking in the glow of his reward for all the hours of study and patience he had invested in me. Those few nautical terms, and the immediate recognition of a mast being complete, were his ROI, or as the business people say, Return On Investment. And I missed it entirely, until years later. He knew that my journey had begun.

Finally my answer came, "Yes, lad, that's where we'll mount the pad eye."

CHAPTER TWO

THE ADVENTURE BEGINS

LAUNCHING

My little sailboat was launched the following Spring with as much fanfare as a nine-year-old boy and a retired sea captain could muster, which, on reflection, was fairly good. The Capt'n had even been able to obtain one of those champagne bottles designed to break on impact, and I was thrilled to have a picture of me shattering it on the first swing over the bow. Then we pushed the boat off the rock and on down into the water.

I held my breath for what seemed like an eternity as the boat entered the water, splashed around some and came to settle right where we had painted the water line. "I think you had better draw breath, lad. No leaks, she's OK."

"Yes sir." I actually exhaled first, but then realized that I needed to draw some air in and sucked it into my oxygen-deprived lungs. "Capt'n, she's afloat!"

"Wasn't that what you and I were planin' on?"

"Well yeah, but, I mean," and here I turned and looked directly into his aquamarine eyes, "We did it! We really did it!" With that I was so overcome I reached out and hugged him, well actually his knees. "This is the greatest thing . . ." I broke off before I let him see me with tears, which at that time I never allowed, especially during beatings. I had made that mistake once after a severe beating and got tagged with the nickname 'crybaby', a few years earlier, and I hated it.

He unwrapped my hands from around him, and kneeled so he could wrap his around me. "I am very proud of you, son." It was the first time he had used that term, and I can't remember ever feeling as good about hearing it used by anyone else. "Now, lets see if she can stand the weight of a couple of sailors, and then we have to run some 'sea trials'. Or in this case, 'cove trials'." He patted me on the shoulder and we withdrew from the hug. And as we did, I could have bet I saw a tear in his eye. But I dismissed it as probably sweat from the launching, old men don't cry.

THE AMBASSADOR

It was at that moment when we both remembered our guest. And with some considerable embarrassment we turned to face the ambassador. Only to find that he had discretely turned to look out over the cove. "Well, you old reprobate fresh water dog, what do you think?" Asked my Captain.

"Don't worry boy, I always consider the source of the comments. And knowing that the salt air over the years has effected his ability to express himself, I simply ignore him." Then he turned to the captain, "And you sir are eminently worth ignoring".

"Yes, well, as you can see this young sailor has at the ripe old age of nine years old done what you river rats have never contemplated. He is a salt water sailor."

"I can see that. The only confusion is how he has done it with you as his teacher." The ambassador came closer to me and reached out his hand to shake mine. "All of this old men stuff aside. Congratulations young man. This really is quite an achievement." He kneeled down and looked me straight in the eye. "I was glad to have a small part in this, but it was you who did the lions share of the work. I am truly amazed at how you have taken to this project."

"Thank you, sir. I don't know what we would have done without your mast though." I had finally learned to accept gratefully generosity on the part of others. "Can you ride with us on the first trials?"

"Why, thank you lad, that is a nice offer. But as you can see, an eight-foot boat is really for one or two. I think I'll let the Captain get wet with you, he keeps on insisting that he is an old salt, after all, and I'll ride another day." Here he reached for the camera on the rock. "Besides, my job as photographer means I should stay on land to get the best shots." He reached out and touched my shoulder. "But it was very nice that you were willing to share this special time with your captain, with me, thank you."

"Only because he doesn't know that river rats melt in sea water." And the captain and the ambassador went into one of their loving tirades.

I had met the ambassador earlier that year only a few days after seeing the mast for the boat the first time. I had gotten into the habit of storming into the captain's home, unannounced, and usually screaming out for him at the top of my lungs. I should add here that back then no one in our neighborhood had locks on the doors of their homes. Everyone simply knew that no one would steal anything, and access was virtually unlimited.

On this particular day while I entered his living room yelling, I noticed that he was sitting with another person, a very distinguished looking other person, and I stopped in my tracks, and shut up abruptly, and began to blush from embarrassment.

"I think this would be your 'little salt', you keep referring to, eh Cap?" And both men rose to their feet.

"Aye, a little more enthusiastic than would seem appropriate." A stern eye leveled on to me, and then turned soft as he turned to the ambassador, "but one who it is my distinct pleasure and privilege to introduce to you, Mr. Ambassador."

"Little Salt, Paul, I would like to introduce you to the honorable Clifton W. Summers, former ambassador to Argentina, distinguished member of his states legislature, Parliamentarian, author . . . ." And then the Captain's countenance took on a somewhat mischievous look as a smile moved his beard almost out of sight, "And fresh water sailor."

The ambassador reached out his hand. And as I crossed the room to shake it I looked him up and down. The first thing that stood out was his bow tie. I don't think in the ensuing years I ever saw him without one on, even on a beach. A three-piece wool suit, highly polished black dress boots (he always said that the only real boots were Wellington), and an overall look of polished sophistication.

He was, like my Captain, thin and tall. His face, while not having the lines of my captain, had the look of someone who had lived fully, and at the same time was somewhat pale in pallor. Overall he was an intimidating presence. But like my captain, when he smiled everything about him became pleasant.

"Nice to meet you sir." I had developed the habit of speaking each and every word carefully, and even practiced things like this before a mirror so I would not embarrass myself, or my captain. And I proceeded with my 'introduction speech' that was one of the ones the Captain had approved for use with adults. "I apologize for my outburst, sir. I hope you can forgive my bad manners. I hope also that you will give me another opportunity to show the good manners I have learned."

"What's this? Cap, you have this lad prepare a speech?" He looked me in the eye. "Lad, an old politician knows a speech when he hears one." He turned on the captain. "And this old sea dog would be just the kind of task master to make a child learn something like that. Especially when he probably has never had the opportunity to meet and greet distinguished personalities, other than myself, of course." And now he looked somewhat proud and smiled knowingly at the Captain. "You can't meet distinguished people at sea."

"Right you are. Only good ones. Which most distinguished ones don't know or understand about." And they were off and running with what I was to come to know as a running battle between a fresh water sailor who turned to politics and a seagoing one who had lived his life on the sea. It was the first time that I learned that rivalries, as often as not, can form the basis of lifelong friendships. I also learned the fine art of craftsmanship of words to insult or compliment, an art that is fairly well lost, but one, which can be mentally challenging, and very entertaining.

So I listened that day, and for so many more as these two old captains tried to hammer each other with the best flow of words and at the same time never insult the other in hurtful ways. Basically they always attacked acts and not the person. A good lesson for all of us.

The ambassador had a home on our street about half way between my captain's and mine. From the street you could only see a square white box that was the garage, as the home went down behind it to conform to the slope of the land.

But when I finally was invited in I discovered a home with wonderful nautical architecture and artifacts, which are better described in the next chapter. Now back to the launching.

SEA TRIALS

The Captain and I had our very first challenge in getting ourselves into the boat. An eight-foot boat with a sail and boom, and two centerboards didn't leave much room for people. But we did manage to place me at the bow for the first 'sea trial', and the Captain did the handling from aft. We soon discovered quite a list of faults and a need for small changes. Our lines for controlling the mast needed to be moved if I was to be able to handle them easily, and the boom raised a little to keep me from having to lower myself to a prone position on tacking. The Captain told me what needed fixing and I proudly wrote notes on the small notebook I now carried with me at all times.

We made a complete circle of the cove and tacked back and forth some more for a better feel of the handling characteristics of the boat and the Captain indicated that we should change places.

I was concerned that if we tried to shift our positions underway that we might swamp the boat, but the Captain said all would be well as long as we agreed what we would do, and carry out our agreements. We lashed the boom amidships and the Captain went up the port side while I headed aft on the starboard side. And I really loved those few nautical terms. I had begun to feel that we enjoyed our own private language or code, which the landlubbers of the world wouldn't understand, and were therefore left out of our fraternity.

I sailed the boat under my Captain's watchful eye, and none too gentle admonitions, for a half hour or so, until he was satisfied that I could handle everything. Then he asked me to head back to the rock, and be let off while I took her out myself.

This was my first feeling of real freedom and control of my environment. I was in charge. I move the rudder, and I went in one direction, I move the boom and I took advantage of a wind and gained speed. It was so exhilarating and at the same time freeing. Then I heard the Captain calling. When I looked he was waiving me toward the rock.

When I arrived he said I should pass him the line we had tied to the top of the mast, and pull a little away from the moorings. He then announced that he was going to pull the boat over on its side, purposefully swamping it. We had agreed to the necessity for this, but I was still nervous about putting her (all boats are referred to in the feminine gender) over on her side on purpose. But the Captain insisted that I would be doing it frequently, and we should know exactly what we would do, and how we would do it in the event of an accidental overturning while sailing.

So, as soon as the Captain felt I was far enough away from our moorings he pulled on the rope until water began to flow over the gunwale and my sailboat whose career at that point was still less than two hours began to sink. Even though I had gone over everything many times with my Captain, and agreed that it was in the interest of safety, that first look at water coming into the boat, first slowly then more rapidly, was very upsetting. "Captain, STOP! We can't do this—it's coming in! Oh Captain, no, don't do it, Please stop!"

The ambassador ran to the Captain, "What on earth has come over you? Can't you see the fear in the boy? Stop this minute!" But my Captain kept on pulling on the rope, and my sailboat kept filling with water. The Ambassador kept imploring my Captain to stop pulling the boat over, and I thought more and more kindly toward him, and confused and scared about my Captain's continuing to sink my sailboat.

"His fear is normal, you river rat. But it is irrational, and must be overcome if he is to ever become a sailor of the seas." And he calmly took another handful of rope and pulled my boat over a little more.

By this time my boat was half full of water and I was getting wet. I had forgotten that I was dressed in dungarees and boat shoes, and shirt, and somehow as the dungarees began to get wet the fear rose within my body paralyzing me. I didn't say anything, no scream, no movement, but totally paralyzing fear had overtaken my every fiber and thought.

"Lad, take a deep breath." I stood still frozen in time and space. "Little Salt! I said take a deep breath!" And my Captain took a loose bite on the rope and flicked it so it hit me on my arm and shoulder. It was as if I were being waken up from an awful nightmare. I looked at my Captain as the water passed over my knees. "This is an adventure boy. Remember what we talked about. Fear is normal, but you can't be normal and achieve extraordinary things. You have to work through the fear." He began to again pull over the boat, and now I began to look at my environment. I took those deep breaths, and I began saying to myself what the Captain had told me and I had repeated until it had become my mantra for this event. "I can swim. I can survive. I can regain control. I can be the master of my fate."

Over and over again as the boat finally went over on her side, and I was sent unceremoniously into the water.

Suddenly I was in the middle of floating debris alongside the boat. And I was again overcome with fear. Swimming and trying to capture the items floating around me while being scared for the boat itself was overwhelming. Then the calm voice of my Captain began to take over and I started to relax and focus my energies on the job at hand.

"OK little salt, put a hand on the boat and relax. You need to get hold of yourself, and rest a little. Remember what we talked about. Even when you overturn on purpose it is difficult for any sailor to handle, and the first few minutes will determine success or failure, so the first important thing is to steady up, and breath deeply, then look around you."

I swam to the back of the boat, held on, breathed deeply, and began to look around. Suddenly I realized the wisdom in what the Captain had made me do. Everything seemed more peaceful when I wasn't struggling with swimming and trying to capture floating items. If the items were floating I could get them once the boat was upright, and do so easier. First things first, I knew the priorities, and needed to fight down the fear, so I could move the priorities to the front of my mind, and attack the situation with confidence. And that meant getting the boat back upright.

"All right, little salt, enough rest. Swim around to the bottom of the boat and get on the centerboard. Good. Now, put your hands on the gunwale and lets see if your weight will put her right."

Try as I might my scrawny body wouldn't provide enough weight to bring the boat back to the upright position.

"Won't work that way, li'l salt, any ideas?"

I looked around for a while. Then I suddenly realized that the farther out on the centerboard I got the more weight I would bring to bear on lifting the mast out of the water. "Captain, I can use the rope from the sheeting lines. If I wrap one end around the oarlock I can back out on the centerboard and put my whole weight at the end."

"Good idea li'l salt, give it a try."

I grabbed the line, wrapped one end around the oarlock, and stood up on the side of the boat, and began backing down the centerboard. When I was at the end of the centerboard I leaned back against the rope, and suddenly I could see the tip of the mast come out of the water. "She's coming up Captain."

"Good work boy. Now, haul yourself in. You will need to keep some weight on her all the way up. Good, keep on hauling yourself toward the boat."

Now my feet and the centerboard were underwater. I kept hauling in on the line and the boat kept rising, and then it was again vertical. But it was full of water.

"That was excellent little salt. Now, go around the stern and unhook the bailing scoop we made."

I swam to the stern and took the bailing scoop we had made off it's mounting. I slipped and lost the handle, and suddenly realized why my captain had insisted that we make the scoop out of wood . . . it floated.

I grabbed the center of the stern with one hand, and the handle of our bailing scoop with the other, reached over and began to remove water.

"Good thinking." Here the Captain couldn't resist chiding the Ambassador a little, "See that you old river rat? Salt water sailors instinctively know not to go to the side and swamp their work."

"Yes you old sea dog, especially when they had been taught to do so by a real sailor from the mightiest river of them all!" Here he looked over the water to me. "Right, little salt?"

And I was caught in the middle of their banter. I thought for only a second and realized that I had but one course open to me and that was honesty. "Yes, sir." I also knew instinctively to keep my part to a respectful few words, and get back to work.

When the boat had risen almost to the water line I jumped into the boat and kept on bailing. "You can finish the rest of the bailing later on, now get on with picking up your flotsam and jetsam. Then lets get a list of what we need to secure better, and how we can plan better for the capsizing you will be doing in the future, lad."

I suddenly remembered my list. I reached into my pocket and pulled out a soggy mess of paper, which I held up to the sky. "I guess the first thing will be to waterproof my lists, Captain!"

I don't know why but that seemed the funniest thing to the three of us, and we all began laughing. One would look at another and the laughter would start all over again, until finally my Captain said, "Gory Be, you are a sight. Now lad, finish your work and tie up the boat so we can dry everything out, and complete the work we discovered on the sea trials."

I lost three more days of sailing while we brought the boat back to the Captain's garage shop and made the little touches which would help in making my seamanship easier. We even created a rope specifically for my use in righting the boat and clip mounted it along the stern for easy access. I think I used that particular rope more than any other over the course of the summer as I tested the limits of the boat and myself.

SHAKEDOWN CRUISING

Once back in the water we began what my Captain called shakedown cruising. We first wrote out a list of goals for sailing the boat which I agreed would be something I would like to do, and we began to test how I would carry out each function. First along side of the dock a 'dry run', and then further out, and finally under actual conditions.

For example, I still wanted to use the boat for my crabbing and catching fish on the cove, and I quickly learned that fishing and crabbing were not easily done from a sailboat without making some adjustments. Nothing we set out to do was particularly difficult, but everything did require skill development and by practicing it in steps my confidence was built up in progressive stages. That way, by the time I was in a moving current with a cross wind blowing me and my little craft around; instead of panicking I knew exactly what I must do to maintain station and achieve my goal of setting the pot, or placing the fishing line exactly where I wanted it.

The amazing thing was that as I progressed through the steps to competence in each and every endeavor required for good seamanship in my rowboat, now a sailboat, I didn't think about having great moments of joy or exhilaration, I just knew and understood that I was able to do more and that I could do things better than I could earlier. Particularly where safety was concerned.

My Captain was always going on about safety. He would take me out in the middle of the cove and have me practice swimming and floating for survival. Eventually I could swim across the cove, and could stay afloat longer than a full hour. My floating was in fact only limited by how much I would begin to look like a prune, or turned blue as the water began to get colder.

The key to everything was always to remain calm. My Captain was forever quoting (actually paraphrasing) Rudyard Kipling's poem IF; "If you can keep your head when all about you are losing theirs, you will win."

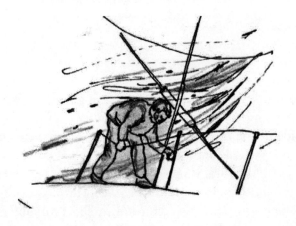

CHAPTER THREE

CONTINUING THE VOYAGE

(COMMISSIONING)

Sailing on the small cove gave me lots of opportunity to reflect on my situation. Most often it seemed hopeless. Abuse in formative years is, well, difficult to handle. Especially when your attacker is a parent, and you are told to respect (as in honor) your father and mother. The conflict in rules and living with the rules can make survival seem impossible, never the less try to keep on growing.

One day I was sailing on the cove, as I often did after a rather severe beating, and had forgotten not only the beating but also the condition it had left me in; severely bruised and even a little bloodied. I was sailing to the rock and my moorings when I heard a familiar voice with an unfamiliar tone . . .

"In the name of Neptune!" I looked up at a vision of rage on my Captain's face, which made me think it was directed at me for some faulty bit of boat handling or other.

"Sorry Captain! I didn't think I was doing it wrong."

"What?"

"I didn't know I would make you angry. Tell me what I did wrong and I'll make it right. I promise."

"Dear God. You think I'm angry at you?"

"Aren't you?"

"No, of course not. I just . . . Well, look, lets tie up the boat before you drift away." And with that we completed the mooring and the Captain became calm once again.

"As Neptune is my witness, boy. And you hear me well lad." He put his hand on my shoulder and the lines in his face formed a map of sadness. "First, don't you ever worry or feel or believe that I could ever be angry with you. OK?"

"Yes, sir." But even as I replied I felt that something was in the air I hadn't discovered yet, and it wasn't good. "It's OK though Capt'n, I'm used to it."

"And that is exactly what I'm angry about."

"Sir."

"What happened to you, son?" Here he looked even sadder and pointed to the bruises and dried blood. "And this time don't tell me you mishandled the boom vang. Rec'n?"

I suddenly realized how bad I looked, but I also knew the admonition that while we were supposed to be receiving the same discipline as all other children, we were not ever allowed to admit that to anyone outside of the family. "Oh, that. That's nothin' Captain."

"I didn't ask you that kind of question boy. I asked you what happened to you, and I also asked you not to tell me a story." His face softened. "It's OK lad, we can keep secrets, can't we? We have been crabbing and sailing two seasons now, haven't we?"

"Yes, sir."

"Well, tell me your secret and it will go no further." He patted my other shoulder. "I promise."

And with that I shared with my Captain the facts surrounding an abusive father (much later I was to learn that he was really a stepfather), most of which he was aware of, but not the degree of violence visited upon my siblings and me. His alcoholic disposition was one of those controlled things whereby he always worked at his job, and submissively gave his paycheck to my mother, and in return she allowed the abuse to continue.

The rationales were many. He had been in the war. Submarines were particularly hard during the war. He did bring home his paycheck. And what would a woman who had two children, then later on four, six, and ultimately eight do if she were to kick him out. But basically my mom got what she wanted, which seemed to be limited to a love life (if the number of children was any indication), financial security, and the fact that in his worst hours (and from our vantage point there were lots of those) he never raised a hand to her in anger, only the children.

But being abused teaches survival skills. I hasten to add not growth skills, just how to survive in a harsh environment, not how to improve your life and lifestyle.

"Boy, we will just have to work around these things. Sort of like the way you sail the cove."

"What do you mean, Captain?"

"Well . . . Let's take a for instance. There are some areas on the cove which are light winds, and some which are heavy winds, right?"

"Yes sir. The Noank side is much more windy than the Mystic side of the cove."

"Well, lad. Do you sail the same on each side."

No sir, wouldn't work.

"Why do you think that is?" And here the Captain settled onto the rock and began with his pipe traditions; letting me know that this would be a lesson important enough that time wasn't a major factor.

"Well . . . If I'm too aggressive on the Noank side I can capsize faster than on the Mystic side. But if I'm not aggressive enough on the Mystic side, like keeping the sheet lines tight enough, then I don't get anywhere. Is that what you mean?"

"Exactly, little salt." The captain again looked at my bruises and dug at his pipe. "You think there might be something to people being the same challenge to your sailing skills?" And here my facial expression must have revealed that my Captain had gone way over my head because he quickly continued. "What I mean lad is that your people skills and your sailing skills might need to be changed for different situations." The Captain drew on the pipe and blew a smoke ring into the air, then looked seriously into my eyes. "Maybe lad we can get this fellow to stop the abuse by treating him differently. Ya rec'n?"

"I don't know Captain. He gets drunk and he needs a target, and I'm the oldest and biggest, so . . ."

"Well lad there is one of the first things we can begin to work on. And that is to make you the least attractive target." More of the pipe work, and some serious concern on his face.

"But then he goes after my sisters." I didn't need to say more. The Captain knew of my protective nature and made the connection immediately.

"Well, maybe that isn't the tack for this course." But then he opened up a smile and with a mischievous twinkle in his eye he added. "There is a tack we can find to handle this fellow better. Ya rec'n?"

And suddenly I knew what he was driving at. "Just like sailing Captain?" More to confirm my understanding than to ask a question. When the Captain nodded slightly, and I knew I was on the right track, I continued. "Change my approach to him from one of fear to one of confidence, like when I first handled the capsizing of the boat!" I suddenly jumped up and slammed one fist into my other open hand. "That way I can keep working on it till I find something that works. And I can keep calm and peaceful under fire." Here I smiled a smile that said I just used one of the Captain's favorite quotes in a new situation.

"Lad, it won't be easy. And there will be setbacks. But when you consider the alternative of living in fear vs. living with faith?!?! Well. I just think you can take this fellow on and win. And I also think you have nothing to lose while trying a new approach to him."

"Two final thoughts Li'l' Salt. First, keep this passage in mind during beatings—This too will pass. Say it often and hard." Then he pointed the pipe at me for emphasis. "And Second, I don't think that I would give him any hint that you are experimenting on him. Ya rec'n?"

I turned my gaze out over the cove and beyond to the Mystic River and the tributary it formed to feed Long Island Sound.

"He'll never know." And that day I began to live life a little freer of the slavery of child abuse. My freedom didn't really come till age 16, and the beatings did continue till then. Not as brutal and not as often because I began the process of studying the two sides of the man, one sober and industrious, the other drunk and violent. And when I sensed the change from one to the other I began to adapt how I reacted to the different types, and the gain was more peace.

One of the best defenses was to help my mother with work around the house. Cleaning, painting, wallpapering, landscaping were all the purview of my mom. The more I helped her the less she tolerated my being abused. When mom intervened the beatings stopped. But you had to earn her intervention.

I also learned to observe and make note of behavior patterns. On weekdays after three quarts or more of beer the stepfather from hell went passively to bed knowing that he had to work the next day. But Friday nights and all day Saturday the beer was mixed with whiskey and that was a toxic brew which normally ended up poisoning the children with pain.

Fortunately for us there wasn't TV until my middle teen years and if we extended our play outdoors long enough, and went to our rooms to study directly after that time we often avoided the most explosive anger being directed at us.

I learned that we were often the targets of opportunity, not really the cause of his anger. The demons in his mental closets were many and very dark. And frankly shouldn't have been any of our concern. But of course they were. And the worst time was the dinner hour.

For most of my youth the dinner hour was an event my mom wanted to make into 'family time', yet more often than not it became the worst time for my siblings and me. I couldn't count the times when he would stick a fork in the back of my hand to keep it in place, pour ketchup on it and begin to cut with a knife saying, "If its on the table it is up for grabs". Early on when something happened to one of us the other siblings used to laugh at his attacks, probably more from relief that we were not the targets. But we learned that silence at the table would keep the anger more in check than any other behavior.

Finally, I stumbled onto something, which made this last and often worst time easier for all of us. To this day I am grateful for the invention of the TV tray. Something as simple as a tray, when coupled with proper encouragement finally had him eating in the family room by himself so he could 'keep informed by not missing the news and eat what he wanted not what the kids were eating'. While we were able to enjoy a meal free of the ever-present danger represented by his being with us.

My machinations to remove him from our dinner hour were not lost on my mom. She was always ready, if we became boisterous, to ask, "Would you like me to invite your father in here?" Which would always be met with silence and an overall improvement in our table manners. And, although damaged and in some ways diminished, we survived.

CHECKLISTS

"You know, Li'l' Salt, navigational skills are not the only ones you need to sail these waters. You'll need to create check lists as well."

"Check lists?"

"Yep. Check lists."

We were on the porch where I had first seen my captain. It was a beautiful summer evening. I had plied the waters the whole day and already turned my catch of crabs and a couple of flounders over to my mom for cooking. And we were enjoying tea with crab cakes, something, which my Captain excelled at preparing. Now that he had enjoyed his limit of one crab cake and half a glass of tea, he settled back and began to fill his pipe to prepare to share another important lesson in sailing through life.

"Lad, have some more of those cakes, don't want them to go to waste now do we?"

"No sir, but Captain why is it that you always only eat one and make so many more and then make sure I eat them?"

"Discipline lad. I need discipline to make sure that I don't get fat on such as these." And he pointed to the crab cakes with his pipe. He gave a half side of his face smile and continued. "Lad, your building bones, and I'm preserving them. Now you eat up while I tell you about checklists. Ya reckon?"

"Yes, sir." Although this was not said with much enthusiasm, I was actually glad to be learning another new lesson and very happy to be devouring the remainder of the crab cakes.

"Check lists are simply lists of things which are of such import that you cannot ever risk forgetting them. Basically they are the foundation of taking a boat on the water, or a ship on the sea." The Captain blew out a smoke ring and continued. "No one really knows who created the first check list Li'l' salt, but I suspect it may have been one of the early Phoenicians or even the Vikings. I can't imagine any sailors being as successful as they were without check lists."

"But here in modern times credit for checklists getting such importance attached to them should probably go to submarines."

With this my head raised and my full attention drew to the lesson. The stepfather from hell had served on submarines during WWII. "Submarines?"

"Yes, submarines. Ya see; submarines are designed to go below the water on purpose." And here he turned back from the sunset to face me more directly. "And if you take a ship below the water you better not do so with a hatch open. Ya rec'n?"

"A hatch open?"

"A hatch, or valve. Anything that lets air into the submarine on the surface, when you dive below the surface, lets water into the boat. And water is the most of which you need the least, unless of course you want to go straight down to Davey Jones Locker."

"Nobody would do that."

"Not on purpose, that's true." Again a floating smoke ring rises to add emphasis to his point. "But happen it has. And more often than it should I'll bet."

"Why, just up to coast off New Hampshire the Squalis sank with all hands because the main induction valve was left open."

The Captain's face took on a sad demeanor. "Only thirty three were saved, rest all died very hard deaths."

"They drounded?"

"Drowned. Li'l Salt. Drowned."

"Yes, sir. They drowned?"

"Aye lad that they did. And it was all avoidable. All they needed do was be more attentive to check lists."

Again his full attention was turned toward me. "OK Li'l Salt. How many steps must you go through each time you want to take your new Explorer out on the cove?"

I began to calculate what I should do before sailing. "I guess nine or ten things."

"And that is exactly why you need checklists lad." He waved to the heavens with his pipe. "If it is nine then it must be exactly nine each and every time. If it is ten it must be ten each and every time. It cannot ever be less than the exact number of steps required for getting ready to sail." He pointed his pipe to the skies directly to make a final point. "It must be exactly right. Every time. Always! No exceptions! Ever!"

"Ever?"

"Ever." The captain smiled. "And the best part is by creating and using check lists you can prepare to sail correctly each and every time. You only need to write out the steps on a sheet of paper with a line next to it and put the list into a plastic holder. Then each time you prepare to sail you only need to mark off each step as complete when you finish and you will always know that you are fully ready to sail."

"Sounds easy Captain. Why didn't those fellas on that submarine do their checklists?"

"Don't rightly know. Arrogance, laziness, some would even say just plain stupid. But whatever the reason was, people paid with their lives. And they did so unnecessarily." He paused for breath. "So lad. I think it is time you got out your pad of paper and pencil and we draw up a checklist for getting Explorer underway."

I knew better than hesitate. I pulled my notebook out of my

back pocket and grabbed a pencil from my shirt and began to record the steps I thought were important to getting my little boat and me ready for sailing on the cove.

Then after what seemed like hundreds of questions from my captain. We did finally develop three specific checklists for operating my boat and catching crabs on our little cove. And thus began a life attraction to and work with checklists of every kind.

SAFETY PRECAUTIONS

I had been operating on the cove for most of the summer, and began to look longingly at the river on the other side. And, of course, that began a pestering of the Captain to 'fix' my sailboat to be able to get outside of my cove. Unfortunately for me the exit under the railroad bridge was so low that even at low tide the bridge hitting their heads would knock down any adult who stood up. With a mast to support my sails I couldn't possibly get under the Railroad Bridge.

"Captain. It sure is nice out on the river. I'll bet I could even get some lobster if I went out there."

"You would need a license to catch lobsters lad. Those lobstermen don't take kindly to those who cut into their trade."

"Oh. Well, I don't need to catch lobsters, but it is nice out there."

"That it is." The Captain blew a smoke ring in the air and turned to me. "Li'l Salt. Speak your piece." He smiled and continued. "Shake the salt from your head, let some oxygen get to your brain, engage your mouth and say what you want to say."

"Well, sir. The Endeavor is fine like she is, but I can't get under the bridge. Can we fix it so I can go under the bridge to sail on the river?" I didn't realize I was leaning forward in my chair and nearly jumping up and down with excitement.

"You seem serious about this Li'l Salt." The Captain put down his pipe, rubbed his hands in his normal manner before taking his afternoon nap, and leaned back in his rocking chair. "This will take some thinking."

I was way ahead of him. "Here is my list of reasons for going on the river, Captain."

That got his attention. "What, your list of reasons?"

"Yes, sir. I have eleven goals for going on the river Captain."

"Eleven goals you say? Now that is worthy of more than normal attention." He reached out toward my list. "Lets have a look at that list."

It seemed like an eternity that the Captain pondered over my list of goals for changing Explorer in a way to get out on the Mystic River.

"Hhmmm, written, specific, positive, personal, and your grammar has come a long way too." He turned to me. "I'm impressed, Li'l Salt. Well done." He paused then looked at the list again. "What's this? A name change? Endeavor?"

"Yes, sir. Once past the railroad bridge we will be on something bigger and will have to endeavor to be better, and I thought . . ."

"Right you are lad. Good choice." Here he brought me back to reality. "Given you want this so much we might be able to do it over the winter and have her ready for next year."

I had matured some so a year didn't seem a lifetime away, but it was still a long way off. "Next year? You sure it will take that long Captain?"

"Would probably require weeks out of the water at a minimum and you wouldn't want to miss the rest of this season. Have to invest more money maybe. Study, for sure. Planning and drawings." The Captain stood up and crossed his patio and looked down on the view of the cove, river, and Long Island Sound beyond. "Only way to make it work is to cut and hinge the mast lad."

"Cut and hinge?"

"Exactly. And I may have the book we will need to begin planning lad. Wait right there." And off he went to his library to launch the rebuilding of my little rowboat turned cove sailboat, which would result in a seaworthy sailboat.

"One of the first things that occurs to me is that when you go out from under that railroad bridge you will change the requirements for emergency and safety equipment, ya reckon?"

"I guess if you say so Captain, I'll believe it."

The Captain looked at me thoughtfully and then smiled. "Thank you Lad. That is a nice compliment." Then he turned back to the book. "The only way we can achieve your goal is to cut the mast so you can lower it to get under the bridge and raise it again so you can raise the sails and enjoy the ride."

"May need a block and tackle to make raising her easier." He shook his head, and continued. "Lots to consider." Then he looked up and smiled. "But I think if we built her in one winter we can sure fix that mast in one winter as well, ya reckon?"

"Yes, sir. Captain I think we can do anything we set our caps for." And I truly believed that we could do great things together. An old man and a child to critical outsiders. But two people with the skills to carry out whatever our plans proved were possible to us. And with the confidence built on the successes we had thus far achieved we embarked on converting the mast, boat, and myself into open water sailing.

If I thought the first winter was difficult I was soon to learn that it had been a walk on the water compared to what we were to engage in that following winter. The step from sailing the sheltered cove to sailing on open water proved to be the biggest undertaking to that point in my short life. And it was such that it also prepared me to sail the open waters of living a full life when I faced adulthood.

Things, which were difficult at one level, became compounded in difficulty with just the addition of a desire to be able to lean the mast over so I could go under the railroad bridge and get out onto the Mystic River. I had been forced to learn about block and tackle to hoist up the sail, rig the boom, and install spreaders, fore and aft mainstays, and all the other myriad needs of making a rowboat into a sailboat. But to make the mast and have it able to be lowered onto the boat and then be raised back up. And to establish this in a manner which would still have the mast strong enough to handle the stress put on it while under full winds created a mathematical and engineering challenge we were to labor under for the entire winter.

Interestingly after all the work was complete and you stepped back to look at the result it was so very simple. Often that is the way of life as well, so much work can go into a solution, which in its final form is so obvious and simple.

THE SCHOOL MARM

It was during this part of my life that I shifted classrooms and began life under the tutelage of Mrs. Brown. I know for those in today's school systems it will seem strange that in the 1950's there were still two room schoolhouses with three grades in each room and only two teachers, but that is exactly what I began my educational experience with. Once housing began to pop up and the population justified it the authorities began to build regional schools and from the latter stages of the sixth grade and beyond we began the shifting process of studies with different teachers.

Having one teacher for several years did have its good points. They knew you and your needs. The disadvantage was that they knew you, and your pranks. And Mrs. Brown had witnessed me from across the hall and was prepared for me the day I arrived. The resulting time under a dunce cap in the corner, stoking the coal stove between the two classrooms, and the countless hours I invested on the chalkboard writing 'I will not . . .' for hundreds of times gave me pause to reflect on this stern creature.

Mrs. Brown was over six feet tall in her high-heeled shoes (even they were stern looking). She was a woman of significant proportions, and one who could literally pick me up and shake me when she felt I had stepped outside the boundaries of proper behavior. She and her husband were also dairy farmers and sometime during my first year in her classroom, when she began to suspect the abuse being heaped on me, she was another adult who took to mentoring me and caring for me in ways available to them within society's limits.

So I would be invited to the farm (a short bike ride from my home) to 'help out' and be awarded with some dairy products (or English lessons) for my effort. Often I would also have some homemade cookies with the milk.

One day while at the farm and working on my homework with Mrs. Brown I impressed her with my advanced knowledge of strengths and measures, and she asked me how I had come by the formulas I was using so well.

I went into a description of my Captain and how he and I had taken a rowboat into a sailboat. Needless to say I went on quite a lot about my Captain. When suddenly Mrs. Brown stood to her full height and looked me in the eye and asked, "Would that be one Captain Josiah T. Armbruster?"

I sensed a level of anger from Mrs. Brown, but I didn't understand why. I still knew that honesty was the best policy. "Yes, ma'am."

"We will never talk of that man again." She began to walk away from me, stopped, and turned to face me. "Agreed?"

"Yes, ma'am."

"That will be all for today." And she withdrew into the farmhouse. Fortunately for me her husband was nearby and came over to sit with me.

"Confused?"

"Yes, sir!"

"Well, it isn't a long story, but it is a sad one."

"I am used to sad, sir."

"Yes lad, I guess you are. And you are also entitled to know why Mrs. Brown is so riled by Captain Armbruster." He positioned himself on the picnic table and began the story. "This goes back almost thirty years, come to think, it may even go back more than that. Anyhow. My good wife and the Captains were roommates in college and were planning their careers as teachers together. Shortly after graduation Liddy met the good Captain and that was the end of that."

"Liddy and the Captain married and she dedicated her life to him. Never had any children like the Missus and me. But that woman worshipped your Captain."

"But why would Mrs. Brown be angry about that?" I asked even more confused than enlightened.

"There's more. But the first thing was that Liddy never entered a classroom after marrying the Captain. And even though they enjoyed tea together occasionally the two ladies relationship never was the same again."

"Anyway, as time went on, Mrs. Brown began to believe that all the time the Captain spent away was so hard on Liddy that it was affecting her health."

Here he pulled a rag out of his coveralls and wiped sweat from his neck and forehead. "So much so that it became her cause."

"She would carry on so about the Captain being gone and it hurting Liddy that it just became awful for everyone. Then when Liddy got sick and died? Well, at the funeral Mrs. Brown accused the Captain of having as much as killed Liddy with his absences."

"Do you think that's true?"

"Lad, I never met a couple who loved each other more than the Captain and his Liddy. No, the captain could never do his Liddy such pain. It was just the nature of his life at sea and Liddy giving up her career to look after her man that got in the craw of Mrs. Brown, I think."

"No matter. She will never have anything to do with him, no matter what." He paused and took on a look of sadness. "Too bad though, I used to enjoy the company of the good offices of the Captain on those times we got together, the four of us."

He rubbed my shoulder. "All this is by way of telling you that it isn't your cause. OK?"

"Yes, sir." With that we went back to the chores. But when Mrs. Brown came back outside with cold water and tea I looked at her with new understanding, and a sudden resolve to bring her and the Captain together. I didn't know how, but I felt that they needed to find a way to understand each other better.

SUPPLIES

"Well lad, what would you do in an emergency on the river?"

"Take breaths, calm down, and collect what I can quickly. Make sure the bailer is still in place, and begin to right the boat."

"Anything else?"

"I don't think so Captain."

"You don't think so. I see. Hmmm. Perhaps that is because we have never run drills to make sure we understand all the things that can happen on the river that we don't face on the cove. Ya reckon?"

I knew that this would result in another trip to the library, and then planning and practicing the things we discovered we needed to know how to handle before I could ever get out onto the river itself. The difference was that now I understood the need for this method of preparation and I didn't resist; well not as much as before.

"We'll need emergency supplies to be in the boat. Flares, bandages, first aid equipment, and more. Even some candy or other type of food for energy, as well as some water to drink."

"Why so much Captain?"

"Well, we always plan for the worst contingency. Ya reckon?"

"Yes, sir. I like the candy part. Oh, and we will need everything waterproofed, right Captain?"

"Right Li'l' Salt, good thinking." He patted me on the head and continued. "Here on the cove, you have a problem, I can see you, and help is never more than part of the cove away. Right?"

"Yes, sir."

"Well sir, on that river everything changes. You could be in trouble and I couldn't even see you. Then help might not arrive right away, and you would have to plan on surviving overnight. Maybe even out on the sound."

"Captain, I won't go on the Sound, I promise."

"Don't make promises you can't keep lad. You may not intend to go out on the sound, but do you think the tides are always going to be your friend? Eh? Not on your life!" He stood to his full height, and shook as if to remove the withering effects of age from his body. "Always remember lad that anything in nature can be a friend or an enemy in the flash of an instant. The sea is a wonderful mistress, but she can also cause heartache and even your death if you're not sharp."

He waved me over to the rail around his veranda. "Look out there lad. See how beautiful and calm it is?"

"Yes, sir."

"Well, think back to last September when there was a hurricane came through. Hurricane Carol. Remember her?"

"I guess so. I remember watching the roof of a house fly by my window."

"Do you remember what the waves of the Mystic River did to that train from Providence?"

"Yes, sir." I looked up into his eyes. "We even took six people who survived into the house. Terrible afraid they were."

"That's right lad. Waves came up and over the train and threw it off of the tracks and into the cove." He placed his hand on my shoulder. "Well, if the waves of the Mystic River can be stirred to do such horrible things, can you imagine how really awful the sea can become?"

"Pretty awful I think."

"In fact lad, so awful that you would not probably survive. So, the first thing is to know enough about the weather that you don't go out when a storm is brewing. Ya, reckon?"

"Yes, sir."

"I'll take that as a promise lad. And I want another one from you. I want you to promise me that you will never untie Endeavor when small craft advisories are up. You promise me that?"

"Soon as I find out what small craft advisories look like, Captain."

"Good point Li'l Salt. I guess it's time we had a lesson in signals and such."

"Yes, sir."

THE FLYING TRASHCANS

The next winter went by rapidly. The classes in school were going better, even though I maintained my familiarity with the coal stove and chalkboard. My newspaper route was prospering, and our plans for putting a hinge in the mast of Endeavor were proceeding well.

Couple of things about that winter did make for some great story telling, and I also became involved in something, which later on I found, became a neighborhood legend.

I was, up until my thirteenth birthday, the shortest kid in my class. I understand fully the effects of bullying on the playground. What the bullies didn't know was that their roughing me up was nothing compared to the beatings I got at home. So, I developed into the scrappiest short kid at school, and definitely not worth messing with for the most part.

I also had a fairly well developed sense of humor, and gift for practical jokes. One day while walking from the Captain's house at the end of our street to our house up nearly at the top I had occasion to smack Mr. Slifton's garbage cans with my Tom Sawyer like walking stick. Unfortunately for me, and ultimately for her, Mrs. Slifton was watching.

She ran out of her home yelling at me to stay where I was. When she arrived at the curb she began to 'enlighten' me. "You young people. Don't you know that when you hit these garbage cans you hurt them? And when you hurt them they don't last as long? And when they don't last as long I have to spend money to buy new ones?"

Not knowing what else to do I took the course that normally worked best with adults. "Yes, ma'am."

She began wagging her finger at me. "Don't you 'yes, ma'am' me you, you, young hoodlum. I've a good mind to make your parents pay me money for the damage you just did."

Here I began to look for any damage a switch of soft wood

could do to her bright aluminum garbage cans (as tall as I was at the time). "I can't see any damage, ma'am."

"Don't you sass me boy! Each time these cans are hit they get older faster. Why . . . No one has an understanding that I am investing in lifting up the neighborhood with these new cans. I want a higher standard here for garbage cans. And I will not tolerate you or any other hooligans lowering the stature of this street. Do you understand me?"

Of course, I had no idea what she was going on about, but I also knew the best way to get out from another adult. "Yes, ma'am. I wish to express my heartfelt regret that I caused you harm, and I will be glad to work off the damages."

"I can't . . . What did you say?"

"I wish to . . ."

"I heard you."

"Yes, ma'am."

"Well. I guess this first time we can forget this. As long as it won't happen again."

"I promise I won't hit your cans again, ma'am. Ever."

"Well. That's more like it. OK, go on home, and mind you never hit these cans again." And she was actually running her hand over the tops, almost caressing them in her sympathy over their being hurt.

For my part I literally ran home. But over the afternoon and early evening her attack on me festered. Eventually I put it all together and came up with a plan, a diabolical plan to be sure, but one that has given lots of laughter ever since. Remember, I was a short kid for less than a dozen years, and that most of our neighborhood had no idea how far my nautical training had progressed.

I collected the equipment I would need from the Captain's garage, and hauled it up to my back yard, and later that night 'raised the neighborhood stature'.

Across the street from the Slifton's was the tallest lot on the street. The Andersen's had a seven foot stone wall up from the street, and had built a three story house on the top of the land behind the wall. Their front yard was the locus for the largest elm tree in the world. Well, my world at the time, which consisted of the neighborhood the school and the territory in between.

In the middle of the night I rose and carried out my mission. I raised the two garbage cans (full of trash) up to the highest reaches of the Andersen's elm tree, where their weight could still be supported, and lashed them in place with, of course, the proper knots. I made sure that I 'did no harm', but those cans at some time before sunrise ended up waving in the branches of an elm tree over the top of the highest home in the neighborhood.

The next day, walking down the street to my home after school, I noticed a very large fire engine with its light flashing. On closer inspection, which all of we children returning from school ran to do, I discovered much to my dismay that they were there to try to get Mrs. Slifton's garbage cans out of the tree. And there were firemen everywhere.

When I arrived on the scene everyone was looking up into that tree. Some of the firemen were in the tree shouting to the ones on the ground that they were too heavy to lower, and would need to raise the hook and ladder up to get them down without damage. What had I done? This was an awesome undertaking! I counted four fire trucks, over twenty firemen, and I don't know how many neighbors out watching. I did notice two things. One Mrs. Slifton was seriously upset, and my Captain had walked up to see what the ruckus was about. And I knew I had the makings of a real problem.

I stayed out of sight for a couple hours on the outskirts of the crowd and avoided any one. Just as the firemen were lowering the last of the cans to the ground and the fire chief was telling his people to pack up and get out of there. I heard my Captain behind me.

"What do you make of this Li'l Salt?"

I jumped a foot in the air and almost had heart failure.

"You alright lad?"

"Yes, sir. Just nervous I guess."

"Bout what lad."

And that is when Mrs. Slifton noticed me. "There he is! He did this! He is the one who put my cans up in that tree!"

Well, the fire chief looked at all three feet of me, then up to the cans being returned to the Slifton yard by four hefty firemen, then to the top of the elm tree and finally back to Mrs. Slifton. "Do you have any idea of just how impossible that would be?"

"He did it. I don't know how, but he did it." She turned from me faced the chief and pointed to me. "Arrest that boy, I want him in jail."

"Please, calm down. I'm not a policeman so I can't arrest anyone. And second, look at him. He isn't even as tall as the cans, and he is scrawny enough that he doesn't weigh as much as the cans empty. Ma'am, I understand your upset, but this is just too much for one day, we'll investigate this later on."

"No!" Then she turned to face me, and the seeds of a legend were planted.

"You tell him you did this! Right now! Go on!"

I had always been cautioned about honesty, and with my Captain next to me I had no choice. "Yes, ma'am." Then I turned to the fire chief, who, I should add was over six feet five inches tall and had muscles stretching his shirt to a limit just short of ripping apart. "I did it sir. I'm sorry, and I'll work off any damages. I promise." While saying it I also recalled the mention of jail and added with fearful trembling, "Please don't send me to jail."

The fire chief was at first astonished at my confession, and then he took on a look of what seemed like anger, and I really knew that I was in trouble, and thought that I was probably on my way to jail. He turned to me and his face turned into kindness. Then he kneeled down on one knee and put a very large hand on my shoulder. "What's your name boy?'

"Paul, sir."

"Well, Paul. You just relax. OK? Nobody is going to jail." With that he ran his hand over my head to mess up my hair. "Especially a young boy as respectful as you are."

The Captain put his hand on my other shoulder. "That he is

Chief, and I can vouch for his character being one of the best in the neighborhood."

"You know this boy?"

"Very well, I'd say." He turned to look down at me. "Quite a little salt." Then back up to the fire Chief. "He is as honest as they come. So if he says he did it I would believe him."

The Chief looked at my Captain, and then at me. "Yea, right." He stood up and turned to face the elm tree, and waved his mighty arm in the air. "And he wrought a miracle!" And the crowd of firemen and neighbors all looked up and began laughing, and the laughter seemed to go on forever.

"Stop it! You have your confession! Somebody call the police and have this hooligan arrested!"

And that, as they say, proved to be the last straw on a very frustrated Fire Chief's back. "Ma'am, I think you should be ashamed. Look at the fear in that boy's eyes! How could you single out a child and force him to confess to something like this."

"What?"

"You heard me. You think I can't tell when a boy is so scared of adults that he will say exactly what he is told? Lady, give me some credit."

"He did it. I know he did it. He just admitted that he did it. What more do you need?"

The rather large Fire Chief put his hands on his hips and looked down at the now shaking Mrs. Slifton. "Lady, I have just spent five hours, with twenty of my best men . . . Men, not little boys! Getting your . . . (here he struggled with himself to regain control) garbage cans down from that tree. And we used almost all of our equipment to get them down. And down is easier than up." He leaned into the air in front of Mrs. Slifton. "Am I making myself clear."

The now cowering Mrs. Slifton uttered her last words on the subject. "But, I know he did it."

"All due respect ma'am. That is simply not possible. And I

will testify to that in court if I have to. This is over. You get my drift? Over, done with. And I never, and I mean never want to hear such an absurd thing as a little boy doing better than twenty firemen." He turned to the firemen. "What are you looking at, pack up and get to the station, before we have a real crisis on our hands." And they scattered in all directions gathering equipment and getting out of the way of the wrath of their Chief.

Meanwhile the Fire Chief turned to me, reached into his shirt pocket and pulled out what turned out to be a business card, and handed it to me. "If anyone ever tries to give you a hard time over this you call me. OK?"

"Yes, sir."

The Fire Chief surveyed the scene once more and shaking his head began to walk to his cruiser. "Now I've seen everything. Damnation! What a waste." And I couldn't make out the rest of his mutterings. But I could tell he was very upset.

The rest of the crowd all began leaving, including the flustered Mrs. Slifton. I noticed that the Captain's hand had stayed on my shoulder throughout, and I turned to face him. "What do I do Captain? They won't believe me."

He patted my shoulder a few times. "Seems like a glass of water is called for, ya reckon?"

"Yes, sir."

When we were settled in his kitchen with glasses of water we began our next lesson. "Well, lad. You did put them up there, didn't you?"

"Yes, sir."

"Why lad?"

"Well, she said she had new cans to raise the stature of the neighborhood, so I thought I could help her raise it even more."

"That so?" The Captain began his pipe ritual while harrumphing to keep himself from laughing. "Mind telling me how you did it?"

"No, sir. It was hard, but I used the block and tackle rig you have with some line and lashing straps." And with that I told the story.

The Captain for his part remained calm only choking on a few of the more humorous moments, and at the end began his summary of the lesson. "Well, seems like this could have gone badly wrong for you, ya reckon?"

"Yes, sir."

"Cost some people a lot of time too."

"Yes, sir. I guess so. But I never thought . . ."

"And maybe that is a problem, lad."

"Sir?"

"Well lad. We talked a lot about lots of things, but one we didn't is the law of unintended consequences."

"Unintended is right."

The Captain couldn't suppress a smile. "Yes, that's right. I'm sure you never intended to cause so much trouble." Here he leaned forward toward me. "Did you ever wonder just how those cans would have to come down?"

I thought about that for a while. "No, sir. I reckon not."

"Well, the next time you venture into one of your famous practical jokes I think you should think through the undoing of the prank, ya reckon?"

"Yes, sir, Captain. But what do I do now?"

"Well, the way I see it, you already confessed, didn't you?"

"Yes, sir."

"And I even backed you up, didn't I?"

I looked into his devilishly smiling eyes. "Yes you did Captain."

"Well, seems to me like when you apologize, and an adult backs you up that's just about all you can do. It's up to the authorities to do with it what they want, ya reckon?"

I began to relax for the first time that day. "Yes, sir!"

"Now, mind you. You were very lucky."

"Yes, sir."

"I think that unless there is anyone to counter that Fire Chief this situation is resolved. And, li'l salt, I don't think anyone will argue with that there Fire Chief." And finally he began to laugh. And laugh. And laugh. And when he would begin to calm down he would slap a knee and recall the size of the cans, or the height of the wall, or the tree, and begin to laugh all over again. It turned into a wonderful time for us together.

I did give the Slifton household a wide berth after that day. But whenever anyone from the neighborhood would see me they would either provide reassurances that they knew I was a good boy and not capable of any wrongdoing, or make a joke of my working a miracle. From that day on I was the center of a lot of attention.

The Captain stood up from his deck chair and walked across his porch to the railing, place on hand on a well-worn area and with the other holding his pipe swept the horizon over the Mystic River and our view of Long Island Sound and the Atlantic beyond. "Out there lad. Aah, now that is for real sailors, lad. Not children or landlubbers."

"I'm not a landlubber, Captain!" This was said, of course without any thought that I could possibly be considered a child.

The Captain turned to me and smiled slightly, "No, I don't think anyone would ever confuse you with a landlubber, lad. I am only saying that the sea can be an awful place to be without being prepared for the worst before you leave this safe harbor. Ya, Reckon?"

"I understand Captain." I turned to look out over the scenic view of the waters leading to the ocean of my dreams. "Someday Captain, I'll be going around the whole planet." A sudden doubt and I looked up to the Captain. "You can go all the way around, like Magellan did, even now, right Captain?"

"Even easier now, Li'l' Salt." And the Captain looked up and out over the Mystic headlands almost wishfully. "I would like to go her one more." Then his demeanor changed and he looked down at me. "Although I guess my voyages of the future will be the ones you make and I witness." Then with that full smile which turned his beard into a road map of pleasure. "Who knows, I may enjoy them more than the ones I did myself."

BACK UP

"What do you think of that Mr. Brown?"

"Little bit of chicanery in that lad." Then he smiled. "I have been known to engage in a bit of that myself. Especially when it was for a good cause." He reached out his hand to mine and we shook on the deal. "And I don't know a better cause than maybe getting those two back together." Then as an afterthought he queried. "When do you plan on doing this?"

"Today, sir."

"OK lad, I'm with you and will support the effort all I can." He looked up and saw Mrs. Brown coming out with our cold water and tea. "Be sharp lad, here she comes." Then he changed voice and took on a look of deep concern and continued. "Right you are lad, that could even be dangerous without an adult you could count on to be a witness."

It worked. Mrs. Brown never could resist trying to save young people from dangerous situations. "What could be dangerous, dear?" She looked at her husband warmly. "And to whom?"

"Why, this little tyke right here. That's who." He reached for his tea and sipped it while letting the impact of possible danger to her little charge work through her mind. "Why, I would even consider it possibly life threatening." He changed his gaze to me. "I am truly sorry that I am too busy to watch over you that day lad."

"What day? Charles Brown, what are you going on about?" She placed her hands on her hips and looked sternly at me. "Are you in trouble again?"

"No Ma'am!" I shook my head as hard as I could. "It is just that I have a row boat that I converted into a sail boat and I was hoping to have an adult or even a couple of them who can swim watch me my first time out. In case, well, you know."

Mr. Brown was warming to the plot. "Yes, lad. That boom you described could knock you out, and (here he shook his sadly) well, I simply don't like to think of the consequences of something like that." He looked up to his wife. "I don't want the boy to go it alone honey, but the farm takes all of me I can give, and more."

"Well, I can swim."

Here Mr. Brown showed his true showmanship. "Oh, lad, I forgot. Mrs. Brown was a champion swimmer in college! She would be perfect." Then he looked downcast. "Oh, but she is too busy to play at lifeguard. And for her to do lifeguard duties for only one child? That would be too much to ask of her. Sorry lad."

"Of course, your right Mr. Brown. I shouldn't have asked you. I'll be OK. I don't think anything will go wrong."

"Now wait just a minute. Mr. Charles Edward Brown, since when do you presuppose to speak for me as to what I will or will not do to protect this young man?" She turned to me, and her demeanor softened. "When do you need me to look after you?"

"I was planning on Monday afternoon after school, Mrs. Brown." I looked down at my hands on the table. "But I know you are busy after school, ma'am."

"Don't you bother yourself even one little bit. I'll watch over you. How long will you need me to be there for you?"

"That's great, ma'am. You know the rock at the end of our road?"

"Yes, I know Beebe Cove very well, dear. I even knew Bradford Beebe, long ago."

"That'll be super, ma'am. I'll have all the lines and everything to shove off after two thirty on Monday, but I'll wait till you get there."

"I'll be there at two thirty, boy, and don't you worry any more about sailing that cove."

"No ma'am, I won't." I looked up and sealed the arrangement. "In fact, with you there I'll feel much safer ma'am."

"Thank you." She turned to her husband. "How could you suggest I should leave this young man to the elements?" And she rose and returned to her kitchen.

The timing of this had to be perfect. I looked down at my Buster Crabbe diving watch and realized it was time to set things into action. "Captain, I forgot we were going to take lines of track on today's sailing, and I always worry about carrying your compass and sextant down here anyway. Could you get them while I shove off?"

"OK, Li'l salt. I may get the camera too. Good day for some action shots with the brownie." He looked down at me. "Now mind you, don't get too frisky till I get in a position to watch."

"Yes, sir." And with that he ambled up the trail to his home. At the same time Mrs. Brown was coming down the public trail to 'lifeguard' for me.

"There you are. My, what a nice job you have done with that little boat." As she looked the boat over she became curious. "Did you do all this work yourself?"

"Oh no ma'am. I had the help of a great sea captain." I suddenly realized that our conversation might have her discover my plot, so I began to shove off. "I'll fill you in when I get back, if you have time, ma'am. I know you are busy, and I want to get this boat tested fully today."

"Very well, lad." She looked up at the sky. "It is a beautiful day for sailing, that's for sure."

"Yes, ma'am. Oh, that chair is for you to sit in if you like."

She looked at the two deck chairs next to each other on the rock. "How thoughtful. Thank you." And she walked to the deck chair and sat down. Now I knew I had all the elements together for the great meeting. She was in the one chair and the Captain had to sit in the other to do the line of sight readings, and I could keep them there for an hour or so at least.

I hovered close enough to the rock to be heard, and when I saw the Captain arriving at the rock I yelled out. "Ahoy Captain." And he looked up while holding the nautical compass and sextant carefully. "The lady on the rock is my teacher, Mrs. Brown. She has agreed to watch over me on this first voyage." And I could see both of their bodies stiffen as they made eye contact. I yelled out one final message, "What a great day. The two most important people in my life are here to help me. I'll be back." With that I grabbed the sheet lines and got out of voice range as fast as I could.

I had sailed around the cove for almost an hour. I had watched the two of them sitting next to each other and alternatively one or the other standing and returning to the chairs, and I knew that it was time I faced what I had to do if this were going to work, so I sailed back to the rock and tied the boat to her moorings. "Well, what do you think Mrs. Brown?"

"I couldn't be more impressed with your seamanship. You are very capable, especially for your first day out."

"First testing day out for line of sight, ma'am. But the Captain here has been working with me for over two years on this boat making it into a real sailboat."

"You don't say." Here she got up. "Good day, Captain." She turned to face me, now that I was also on the rock. "I am very proud of you. I'll see you in school tomorrow?"

"Yes, ma'am. The captain cured me of all those bad habits." Now was the test. "He kept telling me how his wife wouldn't have approved of any sailor who didn't do well in school."

She was taken back by the mention of the captain's wife, and began to rise to her full height. "Yes, well. At least he listened to her occasionally."

The Captain was an innocent in this play of turning hatred into something else. "I listened to Liddy whenever she spoke. She was my partner, my best friend, and my guiding light." The captain had taken on his 'Liddy look' of both Love of life and pain of loss.

"Then why did you kill her?" You could tell as the words left her mouth that Mrs. Brown hadn't intended to say such a thing. But there it was, and once out couldn't be taken back.

"I beg your pardon?"

"No need to beg my pardon. I shouldn't have said that. I'll be leaving now." Nervously she turned to leave.

The captain had risen to his full height and in one of the first times I ever heard his words laced with fury, spoke. "Madam. I don't know where you ever got such a crazy notion, but I can assure you that you are absolutely wrong in accusing me of killing my wife." He crossed his arms. "Dead wrong."

"Oh, you killed her alright. Not in the middle of the night with a weapon. But over hundreds and even thousands of nights when she died a little in your unforgivable absence."

"Unforgivable absence? What in tar-nation are you going on about? I was at sea. Doing my job."

"Doing your job? Doing your job? Being with you mistress."

"Mistress? Where ever did you get such a notion?"

"The Sea, that was your mistress. And you were with her so much that Liddy was left to die of loneliness."

"As Neptune is my witness, you couldn't be more wrong about my life with Liddy."

"You didn't have a life with Liddy! She had a life alone. And it killed her."

"Great Neptune, you didn't know Liddy at all. You never understood her, or for that matter me either."

"As you say. I'm leaving and I will never return, so you needn't bother yourself about my feelings."

"Not that I ever did or ever will." Here the Captain uncrossed his arms and pointed directly at Mrs. Brown. "But lady you are very wrong about Liddy and me."

They both turned away from each other and began to walk toward the separate paths. I began to feel that I had only made matters worse, and was somehow responsible for the recrimination between them. I yelled at the top of my voice. "NO!" And at the same time tripped over one of the lines on the rock, fell back and twisted around so that my head hit a stanchion and I fell into the water as I went unconscious. When I awoke both Mrs. Brown and the captain were over me looking down, and Mrs. Brown was also soaking wet.

"Let's get him up to my place and both of you in some warm blankets."

"Yes, I think he needs to rest some before he is out of the woods."

They each took one arm and slowly walked me up to the Captain's living room where Mrs. Brown began to undress me and wrap towels around me. "Do you have a washer and dryer, Captain?"

"Yes, ma'am. And I have a change of clothes."

"Good, lets get him comfortable and then some tea into him, and I think he will be fine." She pushed some of my hair back from my forehead. "I don't think he'll need stitches, but that is something best left to his mother."

The captain returned with a change of clothes for Mrs. Brown. "What's this?"

"Those were Liddy's. You two were close in size."

"You saved these all these years?"

"Of course. Now you get into those dry clothes before Charles comes for my hide. I'll finish Li'l Salt." Mrs. Brown got up and the Captain pointed. "The bedroom is up the ladder and off to starboard."

Softly now, "I remember where Liddy slept." She looked up as if to say something more, but thought better of it and left to change into dry clothes.

Having spent some time in the captain's home I knew that you couldn't go anywhere without seeing something of Liddy, and I also felt that the longer these two were together the better the chances of overcoming their differences, so I simply didn't get well too soon, and when I could turned the conversation to something positive they each shared. Eventually Mrs. Brown had to leave. But the Captain asked her to wait a minute.

The Captain returned with a faded envelope, which he gave to Mrs. Brown. "I want you to know how Liddy felt when she departed from this life. Take it with you and read it when you can. I would like it back." Mrs. Brown took the letter and the Captain dropped his hand by his side. "I never knew you felt this way. If I had I would have done something sooner. You and Charles were our best friends, our only friends really." And he looked into Mrs. Brown's eyes. "And I miss you both more than I can say." With that he opened the door for Mrs. Brown and she left.

The Captain walked out on his porch to watch Mrs. Brown walk to her car and drive away. Then he returned to me in the living room. "Now, Li'l Salt. Let's see if we can't fix up that scratch so your mom just thinks it's another of your father's memorials to abuse."

RE-COMMISSIONING

The following winter was one of the busiest and happiest of my young life. I still had my newspaper routes and added a new interest in sports, to my already serious time commitment to preparing my sailboat for the open waters of Mystic River and beyond. The Captain, of course, made sure I had plenty to read, and Mrs. Brown was now adding her opinions to my learning processes outside of the classroom.

The happiness began a week after Mr. Brown and I got the two of them together. Mr. Brown had called and said that he could use some help with chores, and when I protested how busy I was he lowered his voice and said, "Lad, I think our project needs your attention." So I was on the backyard picnic table having tea and water when, having been properly prompted, asked if Mrs. Brown had read the Captain's wife's letter. When she said that she had been too busy I volunteered to read it to her, if she would like to see how much my reading had improved. She agreed.

Mr. Brown had secretly read the letter, and had filled me in on the background of it's being written. The Captain was several years beyond normal retirement and was still sailing the seas, even though the war was over and he could have taken leave of his duties. His wife had been told she suffered from a terminal illness and had less than a year to live. The letter was written to the Captain to let him know of her illness and her need for him to return to her.

Reading it to Mrs. Brown was one of the most difficult things I had ever done, but the result was one of the best I could have ever hoped for. It all began on a Saturday morning after Mr. Brown and I had finished the chores and I began to read the letter for Mrs. Brown, which follows.

My Dearest,

This is very difficult for me to write, but I am also not one to mince words. I have a terminal disease and have been given less than a year to live. I have done everything I can to assure myself of the truth of my situation before writing to you my Love. I assure you it is true, and that I need you with me.

I have never asked you to return from the sea for me. The sea has always been a wonderful partner to me in loving you. She always returned you to me happier, healthier, and always more interested in me than when you left. I have gladly shared you with that mistress, and our times together were always made more wonderful for the time apart. But this time things are different.

I fear that if you do not return as soon as you can I will envy each day the sea has you, and I never wish to have all those wonderful years end on such a note. So I ask that you give up the mistress we both Love and be with me in my final hours. I know you will be here as rapidly as you can, and I thank you for that. I also have another request.

Please before you leave the deep blue sea wherever you are, go out on a bridge wing and tell Neptune for me that I will be joining him earlier than I had planned. And that I will look for him to take care of me till you can join us. I ask this because I know that you will be a long time alone here, and I want you to know where I'll be waiting for you.

I know that I may have given the wrong impression over the years with my complaining of your absences. I truly regret some harsh words I used when referencing the sea, and your Neptune. It was only later in life that I realized that she is not just your mistress, but mine as well. I have enjoyed her vicariously through your storytelling. So many wonderful hours we have shared while you regaled me with the stories and lessons you brought back from the seven seas. Now I need them more than ever.

I have had a wonderful life with my Captain. I wouldn't change one minute for any other life. I have *experienced heights others could only dream of, adventures fit for a novel, and a Love other women would die for. You see; I knew that every day at sea your prayers and thoughts always turned to me. And over the years I experienced such wonder and Love that I am fulfilled and ready to meet my maker. I just need to have you be with me for the final act. I know you understand and will be here as I ask.*

Say goodbye to the sea for me sweetheart, and then hurry to my side. For my part I will be praying as usual that your Neptune will grant you smooth sailing and following seas to hasten you back into my arms.

Your devoted wife,
Liddy

When I looked up from concentrating on the reading of the parchment like letter Mrs. Brown, sitting ramrod straight, had tears flowing freely down her face and onto her bodice. "Charles, would you be so kind as to call the Captain and invite him to tea, please."

"Yes, of course." Mr. Brown got up took a few steps toward the house and stopped. "When?"

"Now would be a good time."

"Yes, of course."

The Captain walked up the stairs through the front door held by Mr. Brown and into the living room where Mrs. Brown stood; still crying profusely and without a tissue to stem the tide had wet most of the front of her dress. Needless to say Mr. Brown and I stayed as close to the door as possible without interfering in something, which we knew would be stressful.

"I owe you an apology, Captain Armbruster."

"Not necessary."

"Au contraire, Captain." She began twisting her hands together. "I have been a damn fool! I have let jealousy turn me into a bitter and hateful person, and everyone has suffered." Her sobs were palpable. "But mostly you, and my husband. And I am so sorry."

"Thank you ma'am, but . . ."

"No buts captain. I promise that I will shake this horrible approach to you and everyone else, and go back to the person who Liddy would be proud to know."

"She always was fond of you. I often thought more so than she was of me, in some ways."

"And I sullied her memory with my inexcusable behaviors."

"No. It isn't like that Mrs. Brown."

"Please, at least call me Helen."

The Captain was obviously very awkward about showing emotions. "Helen. Like Liddy I am not much for recriminations. What do you say to shaking hands and forgetting this ever happened?" Then he looked directly into Mrs. Brown's eyes. "Today is a new day."

It was too much for Mrs. Brown. She took the few steps between her and the captain and threw her arms around him. "I loved her like a sister. I just never knew how to tell her."

The captain withdrew himself from her grasp and held her hands in his. "She knew, Helen, she knew."

"Thank you."

Mr. Brown knew a time for ice breaking when he saw it. "How about some tea, everyone?" The two friends, still holding hands and looking into each other's eyes, nodded and smiled. "Well, Butch lets us make some tea."

"Sir, not Butch, please."

"Oh, right. Li'l salt, will you help me make some tea?"

"Yes, sir."

When we got into the kitchen Mr. Brown put one arm on my shoulder and shook hands with the other. "We did some good work today, lad. Some very good work indeed."

READY FOR SEA—SYSTEMS

The learning of patience was reinforced over the entire winter with the fact that it took most of our energies and our skill to cut the mast in a way that would allow it to be lowered to pass under the railroad bridge, yet still have the strength required to handle the stress and pressure generated by the wind in our sails. And yes they were real canvass sails we hoisted up that spring. My Captain had despaired of the converted sheets and worked out an arrangement with a sail maker who worked at the Mystic Seaport Marine Museum.

Mr. Bill Frakes was the lead Chandler and Sail Maker for the restoration project on the whaling ship Charles W. Morgan, and when my Captain began to regale him of the tales of the Li'l Salt and his adventures on Beebe Cove, he became interested in helping out. On a visit to the cove to size up the sailboat and me he decided he could make sails for me from scraps in the chandlery at the seaport.

When the sails were delivered they were prime cut without seams anywhere but those designed for reefing the sail, and even the telltales were tailored for the best reading of the wind. When I first raided the sail and flew across the cove I knew that a master tailored my sail. I was not allowed to pay money for the sail or it's design and construction, but I was encouraged to come to the seaport museum to help in its sewing. And if I were in Love with the promise of the sea before, after several Saturdays in a chandlery and sail loft with those involved in restoring a glorious old whaling boat I was hopelessly and irrevocably a child of the sea thereafter.

The leather, hemp, canvass, fresh cut wood, and metal, which are required to make the parts of a sailing ship, all come together in a salt ladened air to overwhelm the senses. The craftsmanship of each person on their individual part being of not only such high quality, but so perfectly adapted to work together with the other parts made by other craftsman in their own shop was very impressive. Metal workers who knew their finished product would perfectly integrate itself with the wood finished by the carpenters to become a fully functioning block and tackle rig. And when combined with the nautical line from the sail loft it was truly a work of art.

Watching, observing and ultimately assisting these wonderful men gave me the patience to take the entire winter to make the cuts on the mast which would allow it to be raised and lowered.

The mountings for the bolts even had to be recessed so the pressure was on a flat surface and when tightened into place formed an almost tongue and groove effect to make the mast even stronger at the point of fold than anywhere else on it's length.

The Captain, in his usual fashion, set up dozens of drills I had to practice and become proficient at before we could re-commission the boat as worthy of going beyond the railroad bridge to the river and sea beyond. He had a new advocate for safety in Bill. They even placed long sticks in an area of the cove where the current was almost as strong as it would be going under the bridge and I had to navigate through this 'gauntlet' what seemed like hundreds of times before I would be allowed to actually go under the bridge.

The reason for all this, of course, was that I couldn't always time my return to the tides and I needed to be proficient at going under the bridge with the mast and all the sails on deck and using my oar to go through with the tide, against it, or even at slack tide. Bill even took me out on the river in his small Cape Dory eighteen footer and had me handle the boat under his grueling instruction for hours at a time. The more I handled the boat on the river the more I questioned all the concern for safety on the part of my two adult mentors. Until a day in March of that year when I was working at the Chandlery and it became very windy. Bill came into the foundry area and found me. He indicated to the others that it seemed like a day to test a young man who thinks he is a pretty good sailor, and asked what they thought. All eyes were turned on me, and with an almost unified smile spoke the words of my sentence. "Aye, Bill. Sailing in this may be a way to test his salt." And with that Bill and I suited up for a short sail in winds just short of gale force.

I knew from the nautical charts that the Mystic River wasn't that deep, but on that day I couldn't figure out where all the water was coming from to make such awesome waves. Nor could I figure out how they could come from one direction in one moment and another the next. I had always thought that waves all came from the same direction and in a straight line, like British

Soldiers in the Revolutionary War. But these waves were more like the guerrilla volunteers of the colonists. They came from anywhere at any time, with any size weapon to knock you out of your rhythm and out of your boat.

I had seen green water over a handrail, and even waves rough enough to shake my sails from their impact on the hull, but on that day I gained an abiding respect for the sheer unbridled strength of water and wind. I also discovered that sailing under harsh conditions could be very exhausting. And unsettling. And sailing without proper preparation can be a very dangerous thing to do, and not much fun.

I also found that drinking salt water, even in small amounts, is not either very tasty, or healthy. By the end of our hour or so I was vomiting from the salt I had swallowed. Not seasick from motion, which is bad enough, but seasick from trying to swallow the sea.

Finally the day came, shortly after my fourteenth birthday that we held our re-commissioning celebration and I was allowed to go under the bridge and out into the river for the first time.

The weather was perfect. I had selected the outgoing tide as the time to go out, sail on the river for over an hour, and use a slack tide for return. I had my trusty notebook and pencil should I discover anything that I needed to repair or in other ways make better, as well as a lunch and drinking water.

I raised my sail, and to the cheering of my Captain, Mr. & Mrs. Brown and Bill, headed to the railroad bridge that until then had represented the restrictions of childhood placed unfairly upon the man I had become. Now suddenly so alone on the cove I had sailed on for so many hours I felt a different feeling. I suddenly felt a feeling of many feelings coming together all at once. I began to find it hard to breathe. I looked back at the rock and my friends getting smaller, and fear began to clutch at my being.

I noticed that my Captain wasn't on the rock. I looked around and couldn't see him anywhere along the cove. I began to become concerned about things going wrong, and in my fear I didn't watch the tiller properly and almost capsized in calm water on the cove. How stupid. How could I be doing such a silly and unprofessional thing as not paying attention? Concern rose to self-doubt.

Who did I think I was to go on the river by myself and in such a small rowboat? I looked down at my arms, hands and legs. I couldn't believe that I would go to the river of adulthood with such a small, weak and gangly armada as that I saw below my eyes.

I decided to cruise in a circle before going under the bridge. And as I jibed to make the turn I looked up to the Captain's house. The Captain was on his porch deck with his telescope focused on me. The telescope was his largest and tripod mounted. It was the one he used to spot returning ships with and challenged me to read the ships name as soon as I could make them out.

Suddenly it all came together. My Captain was looking at me through the telescope and not his field glasses. The telescope he used for ships from the sea, not boats in a safe harbor. He had rushed up to his deck to let me know that he was watching me become a man, a man of the sea. And I was showing him I was afraid.

While I looked up at him, my Captain stood up straight and tall in his full uniform and saluted me. I smiled and cried at the same time. And I returned his salute. When I dropped my arm he dropped his and returned to the telescope.

I became calm and felt fear flee from me. I felt a surge of enthusiasm and breathed deeply of self-confidence. I had, after all, done all of this before. Then I grabbed the tiller and directed the boat on a path to manhood, under the watchful gaze of my Captain.

Everything I did the rest of that day went perfectly. I approached the bridge and at the proper moment went into the wind and lowered the sail, loosed and pulled the bolts (except one centered on which even had bearings installed to allow for easy raising and lowering of the mast) from the mast and fed line to the lowering line, which also served as the head stay when under sail. I then made sure all of the sail material and my mast were securely tied down and headed for the bridge with my single oar providing the power.

I picked up speed with the outgoing tide and only needed to use the tiller to guide myself through the passage under the bridge, and before I realized it was on the other side of the bridge and still moving forward. I lashed the tiller amidships and began raising the mast. When the mast was fully raised I placed the bolts and tightened them with the wrenches. I clipped the wrenches back in their place and raised the sail.

Suddenly I was in the middle of the Mystic River and sailing on my own. The river traffic was not busy, but there were several other boats I had to deal with and not only follow the rules, but make sure I wouldn't be swamped by the wakes.

I checked my watch after what seemed like a few minutes and found that my designated hours were over and I needed to head back to the cove. The return trip brought home to me the fact that everything was now different. I didn't know or understand the implication of all of it, but as I breathed the free air of the river and sound I knew that something momentous had just happened in my life.

The good and the bad of that would be brought home to me within the next couple of very challenging years.

CHAPTER FOUR

CRUISING

One Saturday morning I was walking down to the end of the street to take stock of my pots and do a little sailing. I noticed police cars outside of the Ambassadors home and a black one labeled Coroner with it's back open. I walked between the cars and when I looked into the Ambassador's garage I saw him hanging from a rope tied to an overhead beam. His was my first death.

The police finally noticed me and one walked over to me and asked if I knew him, and he pointed toward the Ambassador with his pencil.

"Yes, sir."

"Come with me boy, the Captain will want to talk with you."

I followed him while transfixed and staring at the Ambassador hanging so still in the morning light and chill. The Captain was talking with the Ambassador's maid, who had found him earlier that morning. "Captain, I found this boy looking at the scene, and he says he knows the guy."

"Ambassador." I almost whispered.

"What did you say boy." The overweight junior officer seemed to be looking for a slight.

Louder now. "I said Ambassador, not guy. He was an Ambassador!" I turned to look back at the still hanging body. "And he should be treated with more respect."

The Police Captain, seeing the exchange, motioned to the coroner to take down the body. Then he turned to me. "Sorry boy. Sometimes we get caught up in our investigation and forget proper respect. What's your name boy?"

"Paul, sir. I live a few houses from the top of the street. I worked on a sailboat with the Ambassador. He bought me the mast for it, and he is really good friends with my Captain."

"Your Captain?" And that was how I ended up arriving at the Captain's doorstep with police in tow on a beautiful crisp Saturday morning in the late fall of a colorful season.

"Well, little salt. Are the police looking for a character witness?" He looked from me up to the police Captain. "I can tell you he is a character, that's for sure."

"Captain Armbruster, we are here investigating . . ."

"Not yet!" I turned to the police Captain. "Wait a minute, please."

My Captain's demeanor changed instantly to one of serious concern. "Li'l' salt?"

"Captain, it's not about me. May we please go into the living room and sit down?"

"Of course lad. Come on in Officer, and please, make yourself comfortable."

Once we were seated the Captain looked around the room. "Well, little salt, we are all comfortable. Now can you tell me what this is about?"

I looked to the police Captain who seemed to be glad to have someone else share the news, and then directly into the eyes of my Captain. "It's the Ambassador, Captain. He . . ." I looked down at my hands. I couldn't bear the look in the Captains eyes. But I suddenly feared worse letting him worry any longer about what it was. The Captain's health had recently shown to be frailer than he wanted me to know, but I did anyhow. So, I again looked into those wonderful eyes and hit him with a ton of emotional bricks. "The Ambassador is dead, Captain. He hung himself, and we don't know why." I stood up. "Captain, with your permission I'll get some tea for everyone."

The Captain's face had seemed to begin to fall apart, but

when he was faced with social graces he regained some composure. "Yes lad. Please. The Earl Gray, nice and strong."

"Yes, sir. I'll be right back." I took a couple steps toward the kitchen and stopped, turned to face my Captain and said. "The knots were all perfect, sir."

The Captain looked up at me and the emotion of shock, loss, and fear all began to evaporate. I had hit the right note. He smiled, mostly in his eyes, which let me know that he would get through this well. "Thank you little salt. Only you would know how important that would be to me. I'll be fine now. All of them you say?"

"Yes sir, he had even put in a hand hold over the noose to boost himself up high enough to do it right."

"Meticulous in every way. Bless you for that little salt. I never would have known otherwise."

The police captain may have been taken by surprise by the exchange, but he was intuitive enough to let it happen. Then as I left the room I heard him inform my Captain that there had been a note left behind, and the reason he had come with me was that it had been addressed to one Captain Armbruster.

When I returned to the room the police Captain was standing to leave. "Thank you for your help Captain Armbruster. I'll file my report and the attorney's will contact you."

I offered the mug of tea I had prepared for him, but he protested that he needed to get back to the scene. "I'll see him to the door Captain."

"Thank you lad." And the Captain sat down again. He suddenly looked old and tired, and I was worried. I rushed the police Captain to the door and returned to give the Captain his mug of tea. Even though he possessed the finest china the world could produce he insisted on tea in mugs to let the ladies know that this was his house and sipping from china would not be part of his environment.

"Captain, your tea, nice and strong. Just like you asked for."

"Very well." He pointed to a chair next to his. "Please join me."

"Yes, sir." And we sat there in silence drinking our tea for what seemed like an eternity. The silence of the room was so loud that I could hear the waves on the rock below. Well, at least I believed I could. The time passed with our teatime pantomime being carried out in the silence of shock and grieving.

Finally the Captain spoke. "I knew he had cancer, but I didn't know about the TB."

"TB?"

"Tuberculosis. It's a problem of the lungs." He looked up at me. "God awful way to die, lad."

"Yes, sir."

He picked up the note the police had left him. "I have to give this back, but the police fellow was nice enough to leave it with me for now." He placed the note back on the table. "He wasn't a coward, or afraid of the pain lad. He just didn't want to give all his money to doctors who he believed are parasites who suck estates dry trying to keep people alive beyond their useful time." He picked up his tea and sipped at it. "Tea is just right li'l' salt." He leaned back into his chair. "He revised his will." He looked directly at me. "Left everything to me. Asked that I find good charities for most of it and keep what I feel I need."

I knew the Ambassador had children and grandchildren and asked about them. "He felt that leaving them anything would only complicate their already complicated lives." And the silence began to bear down on us again.

The Captain placed his mug on the engraved mug holder and looked up at me. "Little Salt. The way you have handled this has been thoughtful, and with grace and most appreciated. Now, may I ask you a favor?"

"Yes, Captain."

"Good." He leaned over to me and placed his hand on my knee. "Lad, would you get in that boat of yours and go for a sail out to the mouth of the river, maybe even to Abbott's in Noank, and back?"

"Yes, sir. I was going there anyway after I checked our pots."

"No, little salt. No work. The critters in the pots can wait a few hours. I want you to just sail in that boat, back and forth across the mouth of the river and while you are doing it just pray to Neptune on behalf of the Ambassador for me. Keep on sailing until you know that your prayers are heard. Will you do that for me?"

"Yes, sir. But Captain, how will I know the prayers are answered?"

He smiled, took my hand and drew me into a hug. Then he drew back, and messed up my hair. "Trust me. You'll know. By Neptune, if anyone will ever know, you will." Then his look became more serious. "Now, don't you worry about me. I'll be fine." He gave me his knowing look. "Yes, I know I'm not as well as I used to be, and I know you hover over me like I'm an old lady, but I need to be alone now. OK?"

"If you say so Captain. But you won't be going out on the deck to watch me with the telescope, will you? It's pretty cold now, and we haven't moved it up to the Widow's walk yet, or turned on the heat."

"Your as bad as my Liddy was."

I knew that he wouldn't be able to avoid going to the telescope to watch me sailing. Every time I went beyond the railroad bridge I knew that he watched every minute. And I somehow also instinctively knew that he shouldn't do so right now. "I'll just be a minute, Captain."

I didn't ask permission I just went out on the deck and picked up the telescope, carried it up to the enclosed widow's walk, turned on the heat and set the thermostat. When I returned to the living room the Captain was looking at me with a newly strange look. "Little Salt, how tall have you gotten?"

"Sir?"

"How tall are you lad?"

"I don't know, sir."

"You just picked up that telescope like it was a small stick, and just last spring we needed to work together to bring it back down to the deck." He picked up his ever-trusty pipe for his ritual that told me he would be well in my absence the rest of that day. "You seem to have hit a growth spurt lad. I think we may want to keep track of what is happening to you."

"All I know Captain is that I have gotten downright clumsy."

"How so, lad?"

"Lots of ways, sir. Last night when I reached out for the milk my hand seemed to go right through it. Knocked it right over. Don't know why, but everything seems to be kinda out of control."

"Yep, a growth spurt." He smiled at my perplexity. "It's a good thing lad. We'll talk on it when you return." He paused, and then continued. "Doesn't cause you problems sailing, does it?"

"Funny thing, Captain. I don't seem to have problems with the lines or tiller, but lowering and raising the mast I sometimes overreach and stub my fingers on the bolts and such."

"That's Ok." He withdrew his pipe, blew a smoke ring and pointed towards the river. "You go on now. Stop by when you finish and we'll talk of things over a cup of hot chocolate."

"Yes, sir. Just wait till the widow's walk is heated before going up there, Captain."

"Aye, aye, sir."

"I wasn't ordering you . . ."

A big smile tuned the beard into happiness for the first time that morning. "I know you weren't. Now go on before I start calling you little Liddy."

I smiled a big smile. "Aye, aye, Captain."

I finished raising the mast and locked it into place with the bolts. I raised the main sail and the new jib that Bill had made for me and turned starboard to head to the mouth of the river. The Mystic river had one side really developed with yacht clubs, marine yards, and lots of other activities, and for some reason had kept the other side undeveloped marshes. As I headed towards the sea I noticed hunters in the duck blinds in the marsh grasses, and moved closer to the center of the river to avoid any stray buckshot in case some of the hunters were from New York.

We Mystic 'swamp Yankee's' had an understanding that anyone who did something stupid or dangerous was from New York. When someone did something really dumb we would all knowingly look at each other, shake our heads and whisper. "Damn New Yorker. Don't know how they make it." It had gotten so fully developed that if something odd happened and no one was around to blame we just all knew that it had been a New Yorker. So just in case there were New York hunters about, I moved away from the marshes.

This was the first time I had ever just sailed for the sake of sailing, and it proved to be the foundation of something I have treasured throughout my life. It is so fascinating to be on the water in a sailboat without any particular destination and let all of your senses take in the wonder of nature.

The small splashes the waves make lapping on the hull as you cut through them enter your hearing and set a tempo almost akin to a rhythmic beat to breath and live by. After a while on a solitary tack it seems even the birds of the sea sing in unison. Even the sound of the telltales slapping the canvass of the main sail becomes a pattern to relax with.

A strong gust of wind pulls on the mast and the sound of the wooden hull twisting under the increasing stresses adds an almost crescendo like impact. A lessening of the sheets, a touch on the tiller, and the stresses reduce. The hull seems to hum a pleasurable relaxation groaning as it settles onto a better and calmer course.

Soon you are so totally in control of the environment that it is hard to tell where you end and the boat begins. A tug here, a relaxation there, a slight movement on the tiller, and you are the conductor of a symphony of movement, sound, light, smells, and even touch are all brought together in a composition of life. Sailing well is the best expression of living well. Lots of work and lots of practice to achieve those rare moments of tranquility of passage—a journey enjoyed simply for the enjoyment.

And so I prayed and sailed for the better part of that day. Remembering fondly all the experiences I had enjoyed with the Ambassador, and the lessons he had taught me. And I also prayed to Neptune to be patient in looking for the Captain to join him. I needed him with me. I wasn't sure why but I knew that I would need him for a while, so I asked Neptune and Liddy to just wait a little longer and then they could have him for eternity. Then, late in the day, I returned to the rock.

Man was I growing! Near as I could figure it was about eighteen inches in height in eighteen months. And just in time for football to enter my life. I went from the shortest kid in the eighth grade to one of the tallest in the ninth. And even though I was working out I was lanky, and very clumsy for most of that time.

As my body slowed toward the finish of its climb upward things began to come together in some very good ways. I had my rowing of the boat, working out with weights (actually books tied together), biking with the newspapers, and running just because it felt so good. The pace of consistent activities with a physical as well as mental involvement kept my coordination on a near parallel, though lagging, pace with the bone growth. I suffered lots of pain. The bones were growing so fast that my ligaments, tendons and muscles couldn't keep up and the resulting stretching caused many sleepless nights from the knifelike pain at the joints.

In order to take my mind off of the pain I read books. Lots of books! Most were on adventures, particularly any and all related to adventures on and under the sea. We didn't have a TV until almost the end of this period and that was a primitive black and white, which in my view didn't compete favorably with the radio, which included extensive use of my imagination.

Also during this time we had moved from a small two-room school to a large regional school in Groton for the 7th, 8th and 9th grades. It was located in the middle of a WWII Liberty housing project, which was designed for a ten-year use, and is probably still occupied today. The nature of twelve to fifteen year olds brought together in large numbers is violence. And to protect yourself from being on the receiving end of it all the time you joined a gang. My gang experience was limited to a little over a year in a club called the Dukes.

I hadn't told anyone of my involvement in a gang. I instinctively knew that it wasn't something to be proud of. I hid my leather jacket in my school locker and kept weapons in there as well. During the end of the seventh grade several things came together to save me from a potentially dangerous course and set me on a better path. First the football coach had taken an interest in me, and second I almost got caught in a stupid and violent gang fight.

There was a bridge between Groton and New London Connecticut, which was, at that time the largest span in the state. We had people in the gang who were as old as twenty-one and as young as twelve, and you can imagine who was manipulated into doing the most dangerous work. It had been decided that we would fight another gang from New London called the Ravens, and we would have the fight in the middle of the bridge. We were told that the traffic back up would allow us to have the fight without police interference. No one thought about the empty lanes being available for the police to come right up to the top of the bridge, stop the fighting, and arrest us all, because we couldn't get off the bridge.

The weapon I had been given was a chain with several of the end links surfaces sharpened. No sooner had the fight started than I witnessed the damage I could cause. I had whipped the chain around the head of a Raven who was attacking one of our Dukes and pulled it back to me with both hands. The Raven went down and I couldn't make out his features because of all the blood. I dropped the chain in shock and at the same time the police were heading up the empty lanes.

I don't know why but I started to run back to the Groton

side and suddenly I heard my name being called out, actually it was my dreaded family nickname—Butch.

"Butch! Butch, it's me, your Uncle Tom. Get over here!" I ran to his car. "Get in the back seat." When I was seated. "Take off that jacket and put it under my seat. Hurry up!"

While taking off the jacket I noticed blood on my hands and pants. "What about the blood."

His wife, my aunt Rose came to my rescue. "Here we keep moist towels for the babies." She passed one over the seat. "Clean up and put the towel under my seat."

All around us was chaos. Gang members running and the police arresting them, and after what seemed an eternity my Uncle Tom asked. "How did you get into this?"

"If you're not in a gang you are in trouble." I looked down at my hands. "Serious trouble, Uncle Tom. I was getting beat up every day. And when I joined the gang the beatings stopped."

My Uncle Tom, like the rest of the family knew my history. "At school and at home. Must have been tough." He turned around to look me in the eye. "Is this better?"

"No, sir! I really hurt that guy. I didn't know they would be going for so much. They even had zip guns." I began to shake all over. "I just wanted the beatings to stop."

"I know Butch. I know." He turned around to the front of the car. "Lets get through this and we'll talk later." The traffic began to move slowly with the police checking each car. When they got to ours Uncle Tom said they were going to a movie but would probably be too late, and that I was his Nephew and this was to be a birthday treat for me. They let us pass. And I breathed a sigh of relief. The relief was short lived when I realized that we were using the interchange to return to the Groton side of the river.

"Will you tell Dad?"

"For now we'll go to our place and I'll call your mother and let her know you will be staying the night with us. I want to talk with you more before I decide what to do."

"Where are the boys?"

"With a sitter. This was to be our night out."

"I'm sorry."

"It's OK Butch. I went through some of what you're going through. A long time ago." With that the car was silent all the way back to the housing project my Uncle and his family lived in. When we arrived he paid the sitter, called my mom, and while Rose tucked the boys in bed he made coffee for us to talk in the kitchen. And we talked, and talked, and talked.

Finally at some very early hour in the morning my Uncle extracted a promise to get out of the gang, no matter what the cost. And to keep him posted daily on my progress. Any day that went without a phone call would result in my family knowing about the incident, and my involvement in it.

A couple of weeks earlier the football coach had found a way to get me interested in football. He simply looked me up and down in gym class and asked if I had ever thought about playing football. When I gave him a sullen negative reply he simply said. "Probably just as well. It takes guts to play something as tough as football. Not for sissies."

"I'm tough."

"You don't look it. You might get hurt by the other guys."

I had heard someone somewhere give a great reply and I stole it. "I don't get hurt, I give hurt."

The coach looked me up and down. "We'll see about that. Come to tryouts tomorrow after school, and we'll see how tough you really are."

The tryouts revealed just how much I didn't know about team sports, or anything team for that matter. It also showed my scrappy side. When someone outmaneuvering me embarrassed me I attacked him with a street fighters response—quick and dirty, which drew the ire of the other potential players, and the attention of the coach.

We had been allowed to select our desired side of the ball, and I took offense. I was thinking of passing or catching the ball, neither of which I could do well, if at all. So I ended up at Center.

I continued at center for a few days of practice and one scrimmage. I was good at hiking the ball, but I couldn't keep my hands off the other players like I was supposed to. Then on our first Saturday morning practice the coach did a magical thing for me, he asked me to try out for linebacker, as he had too many offensive players and not enough defensive ones.

The coach was the quintessential family man and head coach. Teacher of PE (physical education) and all around nice guy, he was quiet and polite. Until he got on the football field, where he became a tiger intent on destroying an enemy. The metamorphosis was something to watch.

When we arrived at practice he would be quietly smiling and exchanging pleasantries with the other coaches, and within minutes his face was almost beet red with veins popping out on his neck and forehead and the voice took on demonic dimensions if someone did something wrong or badly.

The dad who served as linebacker coach gave me some instructions about my job and position. "You are to find the ball carrier and take him out of the game, but only with a clean hit. Got it?"

"What's a clean hit?"

"You tackle him. That's a clean hit. Got it?"

"Yes, sir."

I lined up on the outside left linebacker spot where I was told and the first run came around my side. I weaved between two blockers and attempted to take the head off of the runner. A quick whistle and a fifteen-yard penalty let me know that wasn't a clean hit. Another run and this time after avoiding the blockers I hit the runner in the chest where I had been told and we went down. Only he didn't get up.

The coach ran over to the guy on the ground to make sure he was OK, and when he was back on his feet came to me, patted me on the shoulder pads and said. "Now that is tackling. Great job! You keep hitting like that and we can take the championship." Then he turned and gave the order that helped the runner decide that day he didn't want to play football anymore. "Lets do that again."

The repeat performance was even more violent, although clean, and the runner had to be helped off the field. The accolades were even better. The coaches began telling the other boys to watch me to learn how to tackle and I was hooked.

I couldn't believe that I finally found a way of fighting back and was getting praised for doing it. The harder I hit people, which was gratifying because of all the violence I had been forced to absorb without being able to respond, the more I was celebrated as a winner. Coupled with my promise to my Uncle Tom to get out of the gang, the time I invested in football helped me to have a reason not to be in the gang.

One of the leaders of the gang took up my cause of being in football and not in the gang when he saw the way I was hitting people and said a former gang member being the hardest hitting guy on the team would help their reputation for toughness. I didn't care what the reasons had to be, I just wanted out, and I wanted into football.

My Captain agreed to come to my first game. It was the only one he would ever attend. He didn't like sports much anyway, and the violence was just something he didn't wish to witness. "Seems good for you Li'l' Salt, but that is an area of your life I won't be involved in, OK?"

"Yes, sir."

"Now go and get all that blood and dirt off of you. And I'll take you home."

"Yes, sir." I was disappointed that my Captain wouldn't be a fan of my hitting people as hard and as often as I could, but I understood and respected his position on violence.

And he respected my need for an outlet. On the way home that day it was quiet for a long while and then my Captain spoke. "Li'l' Salt."

"Yes, sir."

"I want you to know that even though I won't be attending your games I do want to hear how well you are doing." He shifted in his seat a little so he could still watch the road and look occasionally at me. "This is very important for you, isn't it."

I looked up into his eyes. "Yes, Captain." Then down into my hands. "I don't feel so helpless." Then back into his eyes again. "I can fight back, Captain. For the first time in my life, I have a way to hit back." And I smiled. "And I feel like a winner for the first time ever in school. People say hi to me and smile, and it feels good."

"Not everything that feels good is good for you, lad."

"Yes, sir. I know."

"But everything considered. I think this is very good for you."

"Sir?"

"Li'l' Salt, I never want you to grow up to be another Captain Armbruster. I want you to grow up to be the best you that you can become." He looked from the road to me. "And I think that your path will need to have something to deal with all the violence in a productive way. I never had any of that handed to me, so I didn't need to deal with it. But I see what you go through every day, living in fear, frustration and pain; instead of faith, support and Love like I did."

The Captain pulled out his pipe and expertly filled and lit it while holding the steering wheel, drew in a deep breath and let out a smoke ring before continuing. "One thing I want you to promise me, lad."

"Yes, sir."

"I always want to know that you will be playing within the rules and that you are committed to becoming the best you can be at your position." He looked at me. "What did you call it, line sacker?"

I laughed. "No sir, linebacker, Captain. Outside Linebacker."

"Outside Linebacker. Thank you, lad." He took another draw on the pipe. "I want to read in the newspaper that you are the most technically correct, competent and courageous outside linebacker in all of Connecticut someday."

"I don't know, Captain. A lot of guys play football here."

"I don't think any of them use the Library as much as you do. Ya reckon?"

"No sir, I guess not. Nobody goes to the Library like I do." I turned up to the Captain. "You think I can find books on football?"

"Of course you will. And they will help you get better faster than the others. Ya reckon?"

"Yes, sir. If the books have good instructions, and I practice hard and well enough. I think I can get good faster."

"Excellent, Li'l' Salt. Not good, excellent. Ya reckon?"

"Yes, sir. Excellent."

"Do I have your commitment on that?"

"Yes, sir."

"Got your pad with you?"

"Yes, sir." And I reached into my pocket for the notepad and pencil.

"Now, lets write it out as a goal that you can commit yourself to achieving." And the rest of the way back to Warren Avenue we worked out the wording of my goal to commit to becoming excellent at high school football in the position of outside linebacker. We also agreed that going beyond high school with football would interfere with becoming an excellent sailor, and as a result I never envisioned football as anything other than a temporary activity to help me enjoy high school better.

It was just that, as with anything else I got involved with that involved my Captain, goals were the defining step in creating commitment to a course of action. The goals then needed to be broken down into small achievable steps, which could be taken on one at a time.

"Funny thing about this football stuff, lad." He blew out a perfect smoke ring. "When I see you all beaten up and battered badly I won't know if it was football or family."

"Sure you will Captain. If it's football I'll be smiling."

ENTHUSIASM
(THE ESSENCE OF SAILING WELL)

"One of the things I like most about watching you get into something is the unbridled enthusiasm you bring to the doing of it."

"What do you mean Captain?"

"Well, take today for instance." The tried and true pipe rituals for a long story began. "I don't know many young people who will get up at four in the morning, deliver over a hundred newspapers, go to school, stay after for football practice and then still have the energy left to go check the pots we have around the cove, sail over to Noank to sell the catch and arrive here smiling and trying to sell me on taking money from our work together."

"Captain, a deal is a deal. And our six pots were arranged on a 50/50 basis."

"Yes, but I also know that your mom takes half of what you earn."

"Yea, well. That's my problem, not yours."

"Little Salt, I don't think you are paying attention to your grammar as well as you might."

"Sorry, Captain. It's just that you never seem to want anything from our work together after we reach an agreement."

"Lad, I am comfortable. You are the one with your whole life ahead of you, and the portion I refuse is being placed in a savings account isn't it?"

"Yes, of course, Captain."

"Well then, if I were to need some of it I can get it back, couldn't I?"

I knew I was defeated in this argument before it began, the Captain was adamant that his portion of proceeds were to be put into my savings or used to improve Endeavor. "Yes, sir." I felt that this time it would be good to get things out on the table. "But Captain, is there something more to this?"

"More?"

"Yes, sir. Is your refusal because you don't feel I am worthy of legitimate partnership?"

"What's this?" The Captain sat forward in his chair. "Not worthy? Not worthy you say? In the name of Neptune, where on earth did you ever get that idea?"

"I don't know Captain, it just seems like you still think of me as some little kid who needs constant help." I looked up into his eyes. "I can carry my own weight Captain, and I want to feel that our partnership is good for both of us."

"Well, now Neptune is truly laughing." The Captain saw the pained look on my face. "Easy lad. Neptune is laughing with us, not at us." My look changed into a questioning one. "Lad, you have no idea how far you have come in the seven seasons we have worked together. I remember a scrappy little urchin who would take anything from any adult, and now you are worried that I'm not taking my share."

"It doesn't show me respect as an equal partner, Captain."

"Well, now. That's different. Hadn't thought about that aspect of things."

"Captain, I work hard to prove I can handle what we agree on, and when you won't take your share I feel like I'm somehow not rising up to your expectations."

"Little Salt. I owe you an apology." He leaned back on his chair again. "Please forgive me for being so single-minded."

"I didn't mean . . ."

"No. It's OK. Now listen to me, please. This is important." He leaned forward in his chair and pointed at me with his pipe. "It is I who isn't rising up to the expectations, lad. Me and me alone are responsible for this slight to you. And even though I had the best intentions, I did wrong."

"Let's go out on the porch, lad." I enjoyed our 'porch talks' better than any other thing we did together. I always learned something, but more important I would always have my imagination expanded and my dreams enriched by my Captain. "Look out there lad. The sea awaits you, and a wonderful future it will be." He looked back after a while and put his arm on my shoulder. "Lad, I have looked upon all our activities as an opportunity to give back to you a small portion of what you have given, and continue to give to me."

"But that's just it Captain, I haven't been able to give you anything."

"Oh lad, you are so very wrong." He gestured to the deck

chairs and we moved to them. "Li'l' Salt, You have added life to my last years here on earth. And to an old sailor that is priceless." He frowned a little and continued. "But priceless among friends isn't as fulfilling as a true partnership, is it?"

"I guess not sir, at least I don't feel very good about things."

"Ok then, what is today's take?"

"Six dollars and eighty five cents. And your part should be three, forty five."

"Then, kind sir, if you will provide that to me, I shall begin saving it and subsequent deposits for a rainy day."

"Here it is sir." And I handed him the money and felt a resurgence of pride.

"Thank you Captain. I feel better when our partnership is real."

"Do you think we should negotiate your part and what your mom takes from it?"

"No sir, really. That is my problem, not our partnerships."

"OK lad, a deal is a deal." And he looked at me in a very warm and caring way.

"This too adds to the priceless aspect of our work together."

NAVIGATION
(FALLACY OF PERCEPTION & FALLACY OF COMPLETENESS)

My lessons in navigation had begun in the spring of our second year together, and continued unabated throughout all of out time together. The porch of my Captain's house was studied with unerring accuracy thousands of times, and the position was the same each time.

But the variables used to determine the location of the porch on the planet were always different. And the formulas for linking the variables to locate the porch became almost second nature over time. What was at first awkward and difficult later became systemic and logical enough to become almost second nature.

And the vicarious thrill of being able to use a sextant when most kids my age were still attempting to figure out a compass was very satisfying.

My captain would have me take a position fix on one end of the porch and do the calculations, then move to the other end of the porch and do it over again. We would compare morning fixes to evening ones. All the while instilling in me an appreciation for the environment around us being interrelated in magical ways.

"Well done Li'l' Salt. These calculations place this porch in exactly the proper position within Mystic proper."

"After six years of this Captain, I can say with a very high degree of accuracy that this porch is right where we have measured it to be, and probably will be for years to come."

"Do I detect an unrest in that testament?"

"Sorry Captain. It's just that doing this from a boat or a ship would be so much more challenging."

"What would you think you would need to have to do this on Endeavor?"

"What we have right here." And I waved my hand over the tables contents of sextant, compass, almanac, notepaper, chronometer, and charts.

"Well lad, lets consider this." He leaned back and began the pipe ritual, but with a mischievous smile. "I don't think you could work with all this stuff aboard Endeavor, ya reckon?"

"Well, no sir. The sextant alone might swamp her, and I don't have a writing surface. This kind of navigating is best left to ships." Here I looked down at my growing hands. "Endeavor and I don't go anywhere that needs navigating anyway."

"Where did that come from, lad? Why, we have located this porch hundreds of times."

"Thousands."

"Well, lad, there you have it. And I don't think this porch can be accused of sailing anywhere significant."

I smiled. "No, sir, that's for sure." I stood and looked out over the river and sound. "I just would love to take a position over there at MY1, or over there at Hog Island. Or even Abbott's Lobsters. You know, just for something different."

I turned and the Captain was gone. I figured he was on one of his hourly trips to the bathroom, until he returned with a gift-wrapped package, which he placed on the table. "I have been looking for a right time to give you this, Li'l' Salt. And now seems about as good as it will get."

"Well, thanks Captain. But it isn't my birthday or anything."

"No, but we don't need such events to share something with each other, do we?"

"No sir." I went to the table and began to touch the package. "What is it Captain."

"That's why you wrap something lad. Keep people from knowing till they open it. So, why don't you open it and find out."

I unwrapped the package to find a complete navigational kit, in miniature. "Captain, that is the smallest sextant I have ever seen."

"Smallest one I could find, for sure. That is, the smallest I could find that was still brass, and was actually functional and not just decorative."

"It works?"

"Aye, lad. Works fine. Mind you, she won't be as accurate as my Ginger here. Her mirrors are smaller and it will be much more difficult to get good numbers off of that scale on the bottom. Gradients are not as small as on larger models. But I think you can get some good numbers on those positions on the sound you want to calculate, ya reckon?"

"Yes, sir! Thank you, Captain. This is great!"

"Glad you like it. Now mind you'll have to add a bracket mounting to keep it in place when you are sailing. And you'll have to add it to the list of things you have to haul up here each time you sail."

"Yes, sir. I won't mind an extra trip. I already need to make a separate trip just with the oars and gear, because the two sails are heavy enough that I need to carry them by themselves."

"Maybe you can add this to the lightest trip."

"Maybe, but you have to take special care of these navigation tools Captain. Knocking them about could mess with the calibration. Charts and almanac need to be dry and the rest of the gear has to be kept in sharp condition." I looked up into the Captain's smiling face. "What is it Captain."

"Nothing lad. I just really enjoy these moments." He turned to look out over the sound. "Looks like you have time to test out your first position fix lad. I think you should stay on the cove, and get a position on the railroad bridge. Then bring it back here." He turned back to me smiling hugely. "Tell you what. I'll be the Captain of the cove today, and you are the cove's navigator, ya reckon?"

"Captain of the cove?"

"Yes, lad. Captain of the cove. And as my Navigator I expect a position report with full explanation as to how you arrived at the position." He put his hand on my shoulder and continued. "Then when we get the cove down right, we'll do the river. When we have that right the islands and surrounding inlets." He looked up and out over the sound. "And some day in the not too distant future lad, you'll be navigating the sea and you can report your positions to me by mail." Then back to me. "And those letters will be my lifeline to you, wherever you are on Neptune's vast empire." Then back to the harbor. "And that. Lad, will be our crowning achievement." Then slowly back to me, a little sadder. "And then maybe I can join Liddy and Neptune with some really great stories."

I looked up into the peaceful countenance of my Captain. "Is that the way it has to happen?"

"Yes, lad. And someday lad you'll understand that it's a good thing."

"It's not something I want to think about, sir."

"I understand, lad." He stood to his full height and smiled down at me. "Mr. Navigator, as Captain of the cove I would appreciate it if you would get the lead out and provide me with a position fix on our railroad bridge bow, sir. And if you please as close to a noontime fix as possible."

I stood to my full height, suddenly surprised that I was looking almost eye-to-eye with my Captain. "Aye, aye, sir!"

"Carry on, then."

"Aye, sir." And we came to attention, my Captain rendered a snappy salute and I returned it. Then I gathered up the navigation paraphernalia and headed to the cove to take my first position fix on the water.

"Becoming successful at navigating is so much a key to everything, lad." The Captain had gone over everything I had prepared from a week of taking positions in dozens of locations throughout the waters off of Mystic and Noank. "And what most people don't know is that what is difficult at the beginning becomes easier and an almost natural part of sailing or living successfully, when it is practiced to perfection."

"What do you mean, Captain? Are my numbers wrong?"

"No, Li'l' Salt. In fact they are almost perfect." He lifted some of my calculations to look more closely at them. "In fact I would say some of these you have nailed within a matter of meters." He replaced the papers on the table. "No lad, what I marvel at sometimes is that most people don't ever go through the hard part you have gone through to get into good habits which lead to successful achievements."

"Maybe they don't all have a sextant."

"Yes, that's true, but often they don't even have a compass for life."

"I guess I'm lost Captain."

"Maybe an example will help." He pointed out over the cove. "Say you and I were to set sail today from here to London, England."

"Alright. Let's go."

"Aye, now that's a trip." He broke out his pipe and continued while using his pipe as a conductor would to choreograph his words into sentences and those into paragraphs of iambic pentameter. "Well, for almost 99.9 percent of the trip you can't see London, ya reckon?"

I reflected on that for a moment. "You mean physically can't see it?"

"Exactly. But you know some truths and laws, which others have tested and made to work for you, ya reckon?"

"You mean like longitude and latitude?"

"Exactly right. And what else?"

"Well we know that at certain times of the year and a specific place on the ocean the stars line up in a predictable way, so we can get position fixes related to our position on the planet. And again there are books that give us tides, moon positions, sun position, and as long as we know within a certain degree of accuracy we can again plot position."

"And what good is that information to a sailor?"

"What good? Why everything that's all. If I know where I really am as opposed to where I think I am or planned to be, I can deal with reality, and make corrections while they are still small. Captain, you don't need to see where you are going to know how to get there."

"Exactly. And the same is true in life, lad."

"Life? Life is like a sailing trip?"

"Yes, lad, an ocean sailing trip. That it is. For example you have some life goals written down, do you not?"

"Yes, sir, over five hundred like you said I should do."

"Most of them are fairly significant, ya reckon?"

"Yes sir."

"Can you see them?"

"You mean physically see them?" He nodded. "No sir, of course not. Most are years off from now. Buying a home isn't something a kid going on sixteen years old should do. I want to travel first. A lot."

"So, you see, you can't see these destinations in life, but you know some rules and some laws, ya reckon?"

"You mean like buying a home has a process which I can learn when I am ready."

"Almost. At least that is certainly part of it, navigating that is. But there is more to the story, isn't there?"

"Well, yes. I have to prioritize my goals. Just like my newspaper route being built to a level I can sell it at."

"Goodness, watch those dangling participles, lad. The school-marm will have my hide if I let you get away with that kind of English."

"Aye, Captain. Build the newspaper route to a level at which I can sell it."

"That's better, lad. So, in life we have steps to achieve, one at a time and each leading to another point on our journey. Ya reckon?"

"Makes sense to me Captain. And the navigation through life is like navigating across an ocean. Full of things that can go wrong, which we must prepare for before leaving the harbor, and wonderful things that we should enjoy as much as possible."

The Captain gave me a look of admiration. "Add to that the fact that taking fixes keeps you from going too far off course on your journey, either across an ocean, or through a life, and you, as the saying goes, get it."

ADJUSTING TO THE WIND
(TRIMMING THE SAILS &
LUFFING WHEN THINGS GET TOUGH)

In my sixteenth year things took a final and abrupt turn into adulthood. I had begun to become more independent around the home, and my attitude reflected my increasing intolerance of the violence visited upon me by the drunken version of the head of the household. Finally on one occasion when a fist was on it's way to my face I instinctively reached out and grabbed it in mid swing. "I don't want to be hit without knowing what I did."

The shocked look, and the immediate sobering effect on the 'old man' amused and excited me, so I pressed it for all it was worth. "I won't hit you, old man, but you won't hit me without good reason ever again." I released his hand slowly. "Now, just what did I do?"

He dropped his hand to his side and looked at me for a long time. "Never mind, we'll talk about this tonight." He turned and walked away, leaving me puzzled at his not kicking or beating me in some other fashion.

That night he dropped the bomb. "I am not your real father. Your mother was married to another submarine sailor, who died in the war. He was your father. And your name is the same as his was. Paul Emerson. When I adopted you we changed your last name to mine.

This was their attempt to show me how much they had gone out of their way to provide me a home and all the other crap they felt I should be grateful for. What it did for me over the next couple of days was set me free.

I had heard that families repeated the mistakes of their parents, grandparents, and so on. And I had become increasingly concerned that the father's sins would be visited upon me, and my future generations. Now, suddenly, I was free to be whoever I wanted to be. And without knowing it I was already setting on a different path from the stepfather from hell.

Of course within a couple of days, when I had gone through the sea chest of my real fathers past, his pictures, medals, and letters, I ran through the front door of my Captain's home. "I'm adopted, Captain. I'm adopted!"

"What's that lad? Adopted, you say?"

"Yes, sir. And that bastard will never lay a hand on me again."

"Oh lad, your language."

"Sorry, Captain, but he's earned that label." I suddenly realized that the Captain was not looking especially well. "Captain, are you alright?"

"Well, I've been better." He raised himself up into a sitting position on his couch and wrapped a blanket around his shoulders. "It's just a winter cold, lad. I'll be fine. Just now I would like to hear about this adoption thing, ya reckon?"

"In a minute, Captain. First, I'll make you some 'medicinal' tea, and then I'll tell you the story." I took a few steps toward the kitchen. "Oh, here is the picture of my real father." And I carefully handed over the picture to my Captain. "I'll get that tea and be right back."

The Captain looked at the picture and up at me. "Maybe you could use some of that 'medicinal' tea yourself lad, ya reckon?"

I stood and looked at this wonderful man I had come to trust more than any other living being. "Thank you, Captain."

I had been mixing the 'medicinal' tea for my Captain for several winters now, but had never been invited to imbibe with him. The 'medicinal' part was an ounce of rum added to tea with honey and lemon juice. The aroma was wonderful, but with it having alcohol in it I wasn't encouraged to join in before. This was another small step in my being recognized as an emerging future adult.

"Aah, now that's a cure to rival anything Neptune can offer. Thank you lad. It's perfect." He placed his mug back into its holder. "Now, about your discovery."

Over the course of the next several weeks I shared all of what I had learned about my father. He had planned on going to college when his brother Peter had been killed in action on Guam, whereupon he volunteered for Submarine duty and ended up on the last submarine sunk in the war.

The two brothers never saw their twenty-second birthday. I was to learn that this was a habit with previous generations. Their father had died in a U-Boat in WWI and he also had only recently reached majority. In fact for almost seven generations the males of our family found ways to begin families and die young.

"I have some new goals, Captain."

"The kind you would like to share, li'l' salt?"

"Yes, sir. I am not going to get married till after I am twenty two or older, and I am always going to live as if I will die tomorrow."

"Well, I'd say those are more like commitments than goals, ya reckon?"

"What's the difference captain?"

"Good question, lad. A goal is something you set out to achieve. Like a goal of sailing to London." The pipe ritual was in full presentation, and the light in his eye gave me comfort that while teaching the Captain was in better health. "And commitments are the guiding principals you will use to get there. Such as the fact that you will take position fixes every eight hours or more frequently. Does that help?"

"Yes, sir. I have goals to go after. Like going around the world earlier than you did. And my commitment to stay single is one of the requirements I make to create an environment which will help me achieve the goal the way I want."

"Exactly. I readily agree with the staying single thing, lad. But what is this other thing about living as if you will die tomorrow?"

"The way I see it captain is that the trip is the important thing, not the destination. The destination of life is death. And accepting that is the best way to enjoy the trip."

"Wisdom beyond your years." A perfect smoke ring rose toward the chandelier, and the captain looked from it into my eyes. "Perhaps even beyond my years, lad. Only." A long pause ensued. "Only, please don't over learn your lessons."

"Over learn?"

"Yes. Or perhaps I would be clearer by asking that you not become bitter."

VIGILANCE

"The most important work you will ever do in your life, li'l' salt, is that which involves your guarding your attitude."

"My attitude?"

"Yes, li'l' salt, your attitude. The way you mentally approach everything. The feelings and emotions, facts and perceptions you carry around in that incredible mind of yours has a captain of it's own. Your attitude is the captain of your mind and tells it how to approach each and every challenge you have or will ever face." He moved forward on the couch. "Remember my saying once that one of the things I like about you is the enthusiasm you bring to everything you get involved in. Even your humor adds lightness to everything you see. That is an expression of attitude at work."

"Sure, captain. I enjoy most things. But just now I am kinda biting at the bit to get out of that house."

"Well, yes. But you can't for a while yet. And as long as you can't leave there in the present my suggestion is that you focus your energies once again at enjoying what you have and getting on with your journey preparation. And for Neptune's sake stop drinking from the pity pot."

"The pity pot? Is that what I'm doing?"

"Sure seems like it. You have asked more 'what if' question about the past now for over a month, and while some of that is OK, at some point you need to get on with things."

"I see."

"Don't take this harsh, lad. I just miss the fun loving, enthusiastic and talented young man I have been working with for these neigh unto eight years."

"I know Captain. I just want to get on with my life."

"What do you think your doing here?"

"I mean going into submarines and finding out what my dad's life was like."

"Last I heard you needed to be eighteen and have a high school diploma, ya reckon?"

"Yes, sir."

"Well, that alone gives us two more years, ya reckon?"

"Yes, sir."

"Well, lets enjoy the time. What do you say?"

"Yes, sir."

"I did find out that there is a submarine library on the base in Groton."

"A submarine library?"

"That's right. And a pretty good one, from what I was told, maybe we should take some time to go and study your dad and his submarine career, as well as his submarine. Although I can't find a good reason to take a perfectly functioning ship and lower it under water on purpose."

"Boat."

"Oh, yes. Boat."

"Thanks Captain. I would like to know more about my dad, for sure. And I do want to get on with travels."

"Doesn't have anything to do with the Red Wing, does it?"

"Maybe." There had been a wonderful sloop enter the Mystic River one day called the Red Wing. It had been owned and run by George Goble and Derwood Kirby of television fame. They were embarking on a one-year round the world cruise and were looking for a cabin boy. Mr. Kirby, after watching me handle lines and working aboard while alongside, had invited me to apply for the position, which I did. I had qualified in all respects, gotten permission from the school and parents, obtained my school curriculum so I could be taught on board, received the shots required, and my bags were fully packed and ready.

The last minute the stepfather from hell had reversed his previously granted permission. "If he goes away for a full year when he returns we won't be able to control him." What he didn't know was that I already was out from any control he could ever exert, and his keeping me from going on a one year round the world cruise was only sealing his fate with me.

"No sir, that was months ago, and I am OK with that." I looked up and smiled. "It would be easier if Tom Waterman, who did get the job, wasn't sending me postcards from everywhere imaginable."

"Salt in the wound."

"Yeah. But he doesn't intend it that way."

"Still hurts though."

"So, captain, when do we go to the submarine library?"

"How about this weekend?" And true to his word the captain took me to my first of many visits to the submarine library, even though he didn't understand or respect anyone who would intentionally enter Davy Jones Locker. Bad enough you risked it in war if your ship sank, but to do it intentionally, well that was just silly as far as he was concerned.

I had learned quite a lot about my captain's limitations. Mostly from the ambassador before he passed on. I even knew that my captain didn't swim. I still couldn't imagine anyone sailing the seas without learning to swim, but it was a fact that the captain couldn't swim a stroke. Luckily, I guess, they have life jackets. But this, along with other things, was just not important enough to bring up between us. We always had so many other things to work on that it just wasn't a topic we discussed.

What we did discuss a lot was attitude, and how I would need to be vigilant in protecting my positive outlook on life and my future.

CHAPTER FIVE

ENJOYING THE TRIP

"Life is like sailing, 'li'l salt. What is truly wonderful is the journey, not the destination." The pipe ritual let me know I was in for a lesson. "For example when you head out to one of your little islands yonder to take a fix what is it you enjoy most?"

I replied without hesitation. "The feel of everything."

The Captain seemed taken a little by surprise, but recovered quickly. "Go on."

I walked over to the porch's handrail. "I know it's a silly little flat bottom rowboat. But there are times Captain that I feel like I am away from everything here and somewhere else." I turned back to look at him. "I know this may sound weird, but there are times while I am sailing that I believe I become someone else."

I turned back to look out on the inlet of Long Island Sound and it's tributary the Mystic River. "When the conditions are right. And it doesn't happen often, really. But sometimes when I am sailing I can just tell it is going to be something special."

I turned and looked into the Captain's eyes. "You know what I mean, don't you sir?"

He blew a smoke ring and smiled. "Yes I do lad, but I want to hear it told by you. Please, go on." He waved to me with the stem of his pipe. I noticed he seemed chilled so I walked over to where the blankets were placed for such a contingency and put one over his lap and one between his back and the wicker back of his rocker, then around his shoulders. "Thank you lad. Feels good, didn't realize how cold it is just now. Now, please, go on with your story."

"Yes, sir." I paused to gather my thoughts and take a seat opposite from my Captain. "Recently Captain, I am having a harder time fitting this body into that little thing. If I keep on growing I will have to do something."

"Yes, I have realized recently when I watched you in the telescope that you are getting bigger than the boat itself." We both laughed politely as if the air needed refreshing. When we had finished the Captain looked directly at me. "Now lad, let me live your sailing vicariously through your storytelling." He smiled. "Which I may add is getting better and more elaborate with age. Like a fine wine I can enjoy the bouquet of the vintage of each of your stories as it passes over the palette of my mind."

With the captain comfortable and his pipe in possession of a full bowl of tobacco, I began relating my most recent sailing trip. "It was just Saturday last. I had finished baiting the pots in the cove and decided to take a fix on Donkey Island."

"I headed out under the railroad bridge and turned starboard toward the sea. It was a slightly overcast day and the wind was out of the North East at around four knots, gusting to only around seven or eight knots. I had rigged the jib and mainsail, lowered both port and starboard centerboards to the deep water positions, and was cleated off for a half hour or so straight run at the island."

I paused for emphasis, and to make sure I was describing the details necessary to make the story work in the imagination of my Captain. I then leaned back in my deck chair and continued. "Suddenly the sound of the water passing the gunnels changed. It was slight, mind you. But I was tuned into everything and picked up on it easily. With the sound I noticed a filling of the sails and the telltales moved to the horizontal, and I turned to face aft and check out the following winds source of change, but there wasn't anything obvious. No dark cloud or other indicator of conditions going bad on me. So, I just figured Neptune wanted to give me a little ride while I was out there with him."

"I continued on for a few minutes while noticing that my speed had picked up considerably and I was only a few inches from green water over the bow. I reached to reef the mainsail, then thought better of it. I decided that without any storms on the horizon that I could let this go and take it for all I could."

"Soon I was going faster than Voyager had any business going. But here is the strange part. Although the bow was within inches of going green on me, which would surly end up with me under water in seconds, I had a peace and confidence that nothing bad was going to happen. I also realized that this was shaping up as a ride of a lifetime. Oh, and Captain, that it was, in the name of Neptune, that it was."

"I realized that if I was going to live through this trip I would need to get weight aft and get that darned bow up to ride properly. So I moved a few things back with me, and jostled myself into where I was mostly aft and suddenly I noticed that even though I had again picked up some speed the bow was not almost under the water, it was almost out of the water." I began to gesture with my hands as I got caught up in the memory of the sail to Donkey Island. "With the bow up and the wind gaining in speed I grabbed the sheet for the main and pulled her tighter. And that's when I became airborne."

"Airborne?"

"It's the only way I can describe it, Captain. It was as if the boat was going over the top of the water and only the centerboards were cutting into it. And when it happened I started going faster." I was shaking my head to add emphasis. "Mind you, Captain. I was going sailing faster, not stink potter faster. I had the sensation of flying like a bird does, not an airplane. The only noise was the water against the hull." Here I put my hand over my chest. "And I swear to you Captain, it was splashing against the bottom of the boat. Don't ask me how, but it most certainly was. Shortly, even that sound began to disappear and the silence of the day turned everything into almost a slow motion movie the Voyager and I skipping across the top of the water. It was like a rock when you throw it close to the top of the water, Captain. Only Voyager was almost steady in her ride across the cresting surface. And there were no whitecaps anywhere! Just the wind pushing us across the top of the river and out onto where she meets the Sound."

"My breathing steadied with deep breaths of salt laden air filling my lungs. And this great feeling, almost a tingling, came over my whole body. Doctors or scientists may want to give some practical reason, but Captain . . . Well, I believe that I was in the middle of everything coming together to let me experience something special, almost spiritual."

"Neptune at work, 'li'l salt. Neptune at work."

"Yeah, Captain. And he must have had the tiller and the sheets. Because I can't remember doing anything but laying back and looking everywhere and nowhere, all at the same time. It became something like being water when I looked at it, and becoming clouds when I watched them. And for sure Voyager and I, well, I couldn't tell you where I ended and she began, or the other way around."

"Captain, this continued on until I shook myself and looked around to realize that I had gone way beyond the islands. I could even see the NL1 buoy out by the Race way off to my starboard beam." I leaned forward in my seat. "Of course, now I didn't know how to stop it. But I knew that if I continued on I would be in serious trouble. I didn't have enough supplies to last to England, and it seemed like I was being pulled to the waiting arms of the sea."

"I realized that whatever I did I would have to do slowly. Any sudden change in direction would have probably ended with my swamping and sinking the boat. Well sir, I tried first to starboard, towards land, and then to port to get myself off the roller coaster I was ridding, but to no avail. Captain, suddenly it was like being in the grip of destiny. Like Neptune wanted me. And a whole world of thoughts jumped into my mind."

I let my shoulders slump. "It seemed almost hopeless. Then I remembered that the best thing to do when in winds you cannot control is to let out the sails. So I grabbed the two sheets and uncleated them. Then carefully so as not to have the bow head down into the water I let out the jib and main slowly enough to, well, I don't know any other way to describe it than to land back in the water." I looked up into his eyes. "Really Captain, I felt as if Voyager and I landed back in the water." I leaned back into the chair and shook my head slowly. "Then, of course, I thought I would have to tack a thousand times just to get back to the islands." I looked up and smiled to the returning smile of my Captain. "Yes, sir. Then I remembered from all the studies of the area between here and Rhode Island that the islands are kind of in the middle of things and I could do one tack North, North East, and turn around at the last island and come back to West, West South and I could almost make the mouth of the Mystic with only two solid tacks, so that is what I did." The Captain frowned a little. "I know our agreement Captain, but I was already out there, and I only wished to find the fastest way back. And it did prove the best way to go. When I got back to the mouth it took me longer from Noank than it did for all the ocean sailing."

"But lad, the ocean can be an unforgiving mistress. Terrible in her power to push ships about, and you in your little rowboat." He blew a smoke ring. "I don't have such a good position with Neptune that you should push the limit of that boat or your skills."

"I know Captain. I didn't get myself out there on purpose. It just happened in such a wonderful way that I was struck so as to be moved without knowing how far I had sailed." I shook my head again. "Oh Captain! It was such an exhilarating feeling."

"Yes, lad. Life rewards action. And your actions of these past years, and the way you pursue excellence, these things are always rewarded . . . sooner or later. Mind I don't like you going that far with Voyager. But I do understand how the sea can take over and give you the thrill of your life." He pointed his pipe stem at me. "Just remember 'li'l salt that too much of even a great thing can have a dear price if you let it go too far."

"Aye, Captain. I promise to keep my head about me in the future."

LEAVING THE 'SAFE HARBORS'

I suppose that sixteenth year was in so many ways the beginning of my journey through life. With all the preparation my Captain and I had worked on, I was unprepared. With all the practice I had completed, I needed more. With all the skills I had honed to a fine art, I was clumsy, awkward and at times a detriment to the safety of my boat, myself and those who would come to depend upon me. And finally with all the knowledge I had worked so hard to acquire I had an unbelievable level of naïveté about almost everything.

And that, as they say, is how most of us must finally get underway on our life's journey. That last summer with Endeavor was the very best my Captain and I had enjoyed together.

The freedom from beatings I was enjoying for the first time in my life were allowing me to grow both physically and emotionally in ways I hadn't allowed myself to dream of before. I had not only had a tooth knocked out and numerous stitches on quite a few occasions, but the bruises and other accumulated insults to the physical body which didn't show in obvious ways did result in levels of emotional damage to the personality and psychic self concept which would be a constant source of challenges throughout the remainder of my life.

"Free will lad will be your only weapon against that man being in control of who you are every day in the future." He smiled. "That and lots of work, reading, study, and achievement. When you are busy he can't enter into your mind to poison it. He can only affect you in the tired or dark times. And only then when you let him."

I had built three separate newspaper routes up and had others doing almost all of the deliveries while I was primarily engaged in selling new customers and solving problems with unsatisfied ones. That summer I sold all three routes and was removed from the newspaper world forever thereafter.

Our pots were filled to overflowing every time I made my rounds. I even managed to sell off the string of pots to a younger and hungrier fellow. By the end of that summer I was only working on the docks as a 'hand', and the Seaport as a volunteer. And other than sailing for fun I was ready to give my full attention to school activities, especially sports, and preparing myself to enter the submarine service I had come to be so intrigued with.

That fall was a busy storm and hurricane season. I had several times when no sooner had I entered the river and a portion of the sky would turn dark and begin rolling over the area I was heading for forcing me to head back into the cove, tie up and hope for the best. Finally around mid September on a Saturday I was able to clear the river, and move on past Abbott's and the islands of the harbor and into what was essentially the passing of Long Island sound into the Atlantic.

The gentle swells and steady winds were giving me a quiet and reflective sail, and I had been lulled into a lax mental state of just paying attention to the sheets and sails being properly filled. A sudden chill and slacking of the wind drew my attention to the environment outside of my immediate attention. And I saw one of the darkest storm clouds I had ever seen heading in my direction.

The storm seemed to be still quite a few miles away, but also seemed to be traveling very fast in my direction. And it also was a Nor'easter! Coming out of the North East meant two things. First it wasn't a hurricane, which was the good news. Second was that a Nor'easter is a storm which contained everything a hurricane did except an eye of calm, and often did more harm to those on the water than did a hurricane.

I found myself in the path of a very serious storm with winds pushing sixty knots steady and gusting to over a hundred. And I was in an eight-foot rowboat converted into a sailing rowboat. Now almost six feet tall, I was oversized for the boat and gave every appearance that I had been 'stuffed' into it and complicated my boat handling. I looked around for a 'safe harbor' to land in and wait out the storm on land, but there were none that I could make in time.

As I continued to think out possible alternatives and options it became clear that I was in a position that would require my riding out the storm in Endeavor. I made up my mind that I would give it my best shot so I began to ready the boat and myself for what I knew neither of us were capable of doing.

I reefed the mainsail down two positions and also decided to keep up the jib. I could let the jib out completely if I needed, but a little of it may come in handy to keep head way in swells. And as the storm approached I began to realize just how big the swells I would be sailing would be. The closer the storm got the larger the swells appeared and I finally sized them up at between twelve and eighteen feet. I was in trouble . . . serious trouble. I had unwittingly traveled way beyond the safety circle of wisdom during a highly active storm season, and found myself facing a storm generating waves much larger than my boat, and pushing the wind perhaps four times faster than my boat was designed to ride out. "Captain, I wish you were here."

As soon as I thought that I started to laugh at the idea of the Captain being able to fit into the boat with me. Then as I finished the laugh, and while I was still smiling at myself, it suddenly dawned on me that the Captain was with me. He was with me in all the hours he had invested in teaching, coaching, mentoring and in so many other ways preparing me for this enterprise. And with him 'watching' I was determined not to let him down. I had all I needed and I was as prepared as I could ever be. I took one last look around as the storms leading edge closed on my position, then I looked up into the sky above my small craft and prayed. "Lord, this is your sea, and I am your servant. Whatever your will be, I accept with gratitude for your blessings on my life. Thank you Lord for this life and this opportunity." I then looked at the storm, my craft, and the course ahead. I smiled and again looked to the heavens. "And Lord, forgive me, but I am going to do everything I can to enjoy what promises to be the best ride I have ever had. And I intend to cheat Neptune today. I want to share the story of this ride with my Captain this afternoon." One last look aft as the storm came ever so close. And as I grabbed the sheets of the reefed mainsail and let the jib almost all the way out I was overcome be a calm and peaceful feeling which was matched in the intensity I felt committed to surviving the onslaught of the storm.

"May God grant this sailor the skills and . . ." In mid thought I was hit with winds that almost ripped my sails from the mast! Almost at the same time the water rose at the stern to the gunnels with some splashing onto my back. I was suddenly and irrevocably in the hands of the storm.

The first wave almost did me in by driving the bow under. The only saving grace was the little cup of air in the jib, which acted to pull her up enough to keep from going under. Three more times I almost foundered and lost the war with the storm before I was even engaged in it. Then I remembered the times I had been literally launched by the wind so I had been riding on the centerboards and bottom of the boat instead of floundering around with the boats hull almost under water all the time.

I began playing with the sheets to gain speed over the water, and at the same time lowered myself in the back of the boat as much as I could to reduce the drag I represented. Finally, after what seemed like an eternity of near misses Endeavor seemed to pop out of the water and begin to fly across the top of both the crests and valleys of it's frightening waves. Without knowing the term I was surfing a flat-bottomed rowboat across the Mystic area of Long Island Sound heading toward Rhode Island.

In fact I was surfing so fast that if I hit anything at all it would result in the complete destruction of Endeavor and probably not do anything good to my body either. With that dawning realization I stayed beyond the islands and continued on along a line headed toward the coast somewhere between the end of Connecticut and the beginning of Rhode Island.

The thrill I was enjoying is difficult to imagine. Danger, speed, and the thrill of accomplishment were keeping me highly engaged and on the edge of an incredible high of indescribable excitement as I skimmed along the top of the seas foaming surface. After what seemed like hours I began to tire from the continuous boat handling. My arms began to feel as if the muscles had turned to lead and my reactions and timing began to slow down. Then when I had sailed over the crest of a very large wave I reacted so slowly that Endeavor literally dove into the water.

When I maneuvered the boat in a way to stay on the surface I realized that we were over half full of water. I also realized that I only had a few minutes of strength left in me to come to a solution. I rose over a crest without floundering and saw land close by. As I headed back down the wave I saw docks of the Stonington Yacht Club a ways ahead and determined to head into them as the only practical way to end this voyage and have a chance to live.

I don't know how I did it but I managed to move the boat in such a way that all the water was aft around me or splashed over the sides of the boat and out of it. Then I grabbed the sheet lines and got the Endeavor back up on the surface surfing across the top for her last and most glorious sail.

I watched the wave action around the docks I was heading

for from the crests of each wave that brought me closer to them. None of the waves was cresting over the docks, which was good. I began to believe I could crash land Endeavor under the docks, and with luck jump up to the dock decking and run ashore. The plan began to form in my mind that at the last minute I would cause Endeavor to wallow in the water and slowly go under the docks, when I would jump up on the docks and get to dry land as fast as possible.

The plan was a lot more feasible when the docks were a mile off. As I began to close on the docks the distance between the deck of the dock and the top of the waves loomed as an awesome cavern of space, which in all probability I would not be able to cover. The only problem was that there wasn't any other alternative except crashing up on the rocky coast, which would probably get me killed.

I was so busy getting Endeavor lined up with her final engagement with the docks that I didn't notice that some men in rain slickers had come out onto the docks and were getting prepared to try to help me 'land' and maybe even live. And they were gesturing to me that I was to come to where they were standing and pass under them.

I could make out three men on the dock and they had a couple of life rings with lines attached. They were pointing to the rings and demonstrating that I should lock my arms around one of them as I came under the dock. I raised my arm and waved in recognition of their plan, and headed directly at them going very fast.

They say God takes care of drunks and sailors. Well I think in a very short time that day I used up a lifetime of lucky. Endeavor performed perfectly by delivering me to the exact spot on the crest of a wave to be able to grab onto and lock my arms around one of the proffered life rings. Then I jumped out of Endeavor just before the mast hit the dock and began the process of shattering her into driftwood.

The force of the water on me almost tore my arms off, but I would never let go of that life ring. I have for the rest of my adventures at sea used heavy emphasis on the LIFE part of that term. Slowly, almost imperceptibly the men on the dock pulled on the line and hauled me first to the surface where I could breath, then onto the dock where they hastily ushered me to dry land and into the Yacht Club buildings proper. At one point I turned to look for Endeavor. And I watched as she threw herself, with a final display of dignity, onto a large boulder and shattered apart. The sound of her destruction came to me over the noise of the angry sea, and I was infused with the pain of her demise, and yet the glory of her finish.

Other flat bottom boats may have ended their service by rotting in tepid backwaters, or worse. But Endeavor had gone out in a final blast of glory against the rocks and shoals of the seas coastal targets, and she had done so only after safely delivering me into the arms of my saving sailors. When the sound of her destruction passed through me it was as if everything became silent. The fury of the storm, which had tried so hard to bring me to Davy Jones Locker, abated and the wave that slaughtered Endeavor was the last one that size. It was as if Neptune, realizing that the battle was over let the sea subside and the wind return to normal and the silence became something almost too loud to believe. And in the midst of all the peace and quiet the pieces of what was once Endeavor moved in and out from the rocky coast in her death throws.

Once inside I was treated to warm blankets and new dry clothes and allowed to make some phone calls. My first, and only, call was to my Captain.

"Captain?"

"Li'l Salt?"

"Yes, sir."

"Thanks be to Neptune. Where are you lad?"

"At the Stonington Yacht Club, sir."

"Are you alright lad?"

"Yes, sir." A pause. "But Captain, Endeavors gone."

"Yes, lad. I watched you as you passed outside the islands. She looked like she was flying to her end."

"She truly did sail like never before."

"Lad, I can't recall ever seeing anything like what you just did. Ever!"

"It was pretty exciting, that's for sure."

"Well, I hope you got it all out of your system, I don't wish to watch something like that ever again."

"Yes, sir."

"Is the Commodore of the yacht club there?"

"I don't know, sir. Just a minute." I placed my hand over the speaker part of the phone and called out. "Is the Commodore here?"

"That would be me, lad." An elderly man with white hair who was attired in a blue blazer with the clubs logo on the pocket stood up. "May I help you?"

"Just a minute sir." Then back into the phone. "Yes, Captain. The Commodore is here."

"Good, li'l salt. Please ask him to come to the phone. I would like to talk with him."

"Yes, sir." A pause. "Captain?"

"Yes, lad?"

"You aren't angry with me are you?"

"No lad. I'm not angry. Just a little in shock. I'll be fine."

"Yes, sir. I didn't mean to upset you I just wanted to let

someone know how great it was to sail. And also to let you know I was safe."

"Thank you li'l salt. We'll talk later. Just now put the Commodore on the line."

"Yes, sir." I handed the phone to the arriving Commodore. "Captain Armbruster would like to talk with you sir."

"Armbruster? There can be only one of those old reprobates left on this planet." He took the phone. "Was it you? You old sea dog, who taught this lad here to sail?" Then after a pause, he continued. "Just as I thought. Never saw the like of it Armbruster. And he looks like nothing more than a child! None of my mates can figure out how he did it."

The Commodore and the Captain talked on for a few minutes than he hung up. "Well lad, seems like old Armbruster is insisting that I bring you to him. Says he'll pay me for it, old goat insult me like that." He looked directly at me. "Son, do you have any idea what you did here today."

I looked up at the nattily dressed Commodore. "Lost my boat."

The Commodore looked around him and first he then all the others gathered around began to laugh. The laughter rose to a crescendo and tears flowed from the eyes while they all continued to roll on. Finally they would begin to quiet down and someone would say between laughs. "Lost my boat. LOST MY BOAT! God that's funny."

When everyone had about played out the joke the Commodore looked seriously at me for a moment. "Lad. I'm sorry. Have you eaten?"

"Not since breakfast. What time is it anyway?"

"WHAT TIME IS IT?" And another protracted round of laughter began.

"It's after 1400 hours lad." He turned to someone in a white uniform. "James, whip up a lunch for the lad before he starves to death."

"Yes, sir. Right away, sir." And Jim, whoever he was, walked off muttering to himself my comment about losing my boat and shaking his head.

"We'll get something into you and then I'll drive you over to the Armbruster place." The Commodore sat down opposite me on a picnic like table. "Lad, you may not realize it, but you sailed across those waters faster than anything I had ever witnessed." He began rubbing his huge hands together. "We almost didn't have time to react and prepare our little welcoming party."

"How did you come to know Captain Armbruster?"

"It's kinda a long story, sir."

"I have some time, young man. Especially for something like this."

So throughout my meal I regaled the Commodore with some of the exploits my Captain and I had enjoyed, and how he had taught me to sail and navigate. Then the Commodore began to tell me of his knowledge of my Captain.

"I was in the Navy on aircraft carriers during The War. I didn't know the Captain personally at first, just by reputation. He skippered ammunition supply ships in the Pacific Theater during The War. And his reputation was one of a fellow who was fearless in the face of the enemy and in the case of the odds being stacked against him."

"Early on in the war we had to have ammunition taken directly from Armbruster and his ship. Mind you we didn't often deal with Merchant Marine ships. They normally dropped their cargos on docks in Hawaii and we put them aboard US Navy ships for transfer at sea to our warships. But the war put us in a pickle early on, and the Merchants came through in ways that continually surprised us."

"That time when ole Armbruster came alongside it was in a state four sea. The differential of how our two ships rode those waves was awesome. But Armbruster kept that lady alongside for over nine hours while we transferred all the ammunition we needed for our aircraft and self defense." He looked down at me. "Probably even a better bit of sailing than I witnessed at your hand today."

"Anyway we came to know both Armbruster and his Liddy very well after the war. He began working just regular shipping, and I was pushing a desk by that time so we got together for dinner and other engagements. Long story short he is one of the finest sailors I have ever known." He stood up and straightened out his jacket. "And from what I witnessed today he is also a great teacher."

"I hope you let him know that, sir. Right now I'm a little concerned that I may be on the receiving end of a rather serious lecture."

"We'll have none of that. Why, by the time I'm done telling old Armbruster what you did he may want to pin one of his many medals on you." He looked at the table. "Have you had enough of that there ice cream to eat?"

"Yes, sir."

"Well, then I guess we need to get on the next phase of this little adventure."

And we left the club to go to my Captain's home, where I was still pretty sure I would be facing some adverse consequences.

CHAPTER SIX

REACHING DESTINATIONS

The loss of Endeavor was staggering to me. I hadn't realized how much I had come to be a part of that boat. I identified myself as part of her, and suddenly I had also lost my mode of transportation to work on the docks and Abbott's Lobsters. I was kept pretty busy by events around the loss of the boat by the sailors of the yacht club, and even my Captain attended some of the various ceremonies those folks conjured up for me.

First they had recovered my sextant and some other small items from the water in front of their club. When told by my Captain that it was part of his navigating kit he had given me they built a completely new one and held a dinner where the stories of my voyage grew larger and more successful throughout the evening. So much so that at one point my Captain leaned over to me and whispered. "Li'l salt, if I didn't know better I would think I was in the company of a legend." He leaned back and smiled widely. "Or at least a young man who is on the way to becoming one."

"Awe Captain. I didn't ask for all this."

"Aye lad, and that's the good of it."

Then the presentation of my kit was announced, and I was asked to make an acceptance speech. I turned to the assembled group of sailors and their dates and looked down at the kit and up at my Captain sitting on the dais and said. "Thank you for this gift. I guess I'll have to find a boat to wrap around it." And I sat down.

The Commodore took the microphone and said. "If he can make speeches that short we'll have to have him back." Then he started the applause, which seemed to go on forever. It was my first black tie event and I loved being the center of attention, although I would never admit it to my Captain. It was a great evening.

But being without a boat was seriously working on me. My mother solved the transportation issue by selling me the oldest 'family' car for fifty dollars. It was a very old Nash Rambler, but it worked and I was able to get to where I needed to be for sports and work on the docks.

My second outing at the yacht club was a presentation of some of the planking from Endeavor, which had been made into a plaque to commemorate the date and time I was hauled out of the waters that fateful day when Endeavor ceased to be. My Captain drove me to the event and back even though I protested that I could drive us. "Li'l salt, you're good sailor. I believe you will be a great sailor someday. But I'll drive the car for now." And I let it rest.

One Saturday morning soon after my Captain had asked that I join him in the morning, which I did. "Lets go for a ride in my car."

"Yes, sir."

We arrived at the docks in Mystic and walked over to a slip with a new Cape Dory eighteen and a half footer moored alongside. "What do you think of her, li'l salt?"

"She is mighty good Captain. And the Cape Dory people make a fine hull. I prefer the lines for handling you find on the cruising O'Day boats. But this little gal is just fine."

"Glad you think so. I just bought her."

"Wow! That's great Captain." I suddenly had second thoughts of my Captain's declining health and how much it took to handle that particular boat. "Captain, are you sure you want to sail on this lady?"

"No, li'l salt. I neither want or can sail this little lady, I just wish to own her."

"Why would you want to do that Captain?" I watched his smile cross his face and I knew that he had bought this boat for me.

"Well, li'l salt. Do you think you could keep her hull clean for me?"

"Hull clean?"

"You know. A little lady like this needs sailing. If she stays tied up she'll grow grass and slow down something awful."

"But Captain, I couldn't afford to even rent her from you."

"I didn't say I was chartering her out lad. I just need you to keep her hull clean for me. You wouldn't charge me for that now would you?"

"Of course not Captain. Never. I just. That is, I couldn't."

The Captain came over to me and placed his arm around my shoulder. "We have another summer, maybe two before you move on. I just couldn't tolerate it without your sailing these waters, ya recon?"

"Oh Captain, she's beautiful. But."

"No butts little salt. When you leave I'll sell her and probably make money, the way you take care of a craft."

"I would certainly treat her the best I can."

"Well, now that we have that settled I have one problem I need your help on."

"What's that Captain?"

"Her name lad. I don't think Endeavor will do for any other craft we are a part of. Do you?"

"No sir. There was only one Endeavor." I walked along the boat from bow to stern and then looked up at my Captain. "Quest, Captain. She should be called Quest."

"Nice. Good start but needs more. How about Life Quest?"

"Not on the water Captain." I looked down the river and up at the clear and sunny sky above. "Sun Quest Captain. That would be better at a marina and at sea."

"What about Sea Quest lad?"

I looked at my captain with a confidence that I didn't understand and softly finished the search for the proper name. "Captain, she rests in the sea already, she doesn't need it as a quest. Like all small boats she needs to quest for basking in sunlight to journey on the water." I looked over at the boat again. "She has no business questing for the sea as she can never cross such a revered, loving and dangerous thing. But every night she must quest for the light of day to cross her decks and bring her to life, even if only for a few hours. Then she must return to her dock before nightfall and quest for the rising sun to free her once again."

My Captain placed his hand on my shoulder. "Lad that may be one of the most wonderful thoughts I have ever heard you express. Yet it seems so sad in the way it places limits on this here lady." He blew out a smoke ring and continued. "This here lady is fully capable of crossing the Atlantic, or any other ocean for that matter. And mark my word, sailors have done so in boats her size or even smaller long ago, and will again. I hasten to add many have also died in the attempt when Neptune didn't cooperate."

"So, you shall have your name—Sun Quest—just never doubt that this little lady, like you, is possible of great things."

"Aye, Captain." I looked back to him. "Are you up for a shake down cruise?"

"Aye to that lad." His look took on a sadden disposition. "Afraid that I'll not be much good to you except as handling sheets and such. Not as mobile as I used to be."

"You can see she is set up for a single handling, Captain. You just relax and enjoy the trip." I smiled. "Course I expect that enjoyment just might include some critique about a questionable skill I may have learned from the Ambassador."

"I have noticed some of those coarsened freshwater habits creeping into your sailing lad. And I had intended to cover some of those in our dialogues. Now that you mention it this may be an excellent opportunity to divest you of some of those shallow water habits and replace them with deepwater sailing skills."

"I would assume that you have already had the yard mount the checklists. May I convert that assumption to fact?"

"Aye that you may. Starboard bulkhead aft of the chart table."

"Then with your permission Captain I will complete the checklists for getting underway, and make Sun Quest ready in all respects for your inspection."

"Aye mate. Make it so."

With that little exchange I entered into the world of adulthood with my Captain. I would always be 'li'l salt' but more and more often I was addressed as an equal on the water.

PREPARING FOR SUCCESS

It may have been my imagination over the next two years, but the Captain seemed to come to life each time we took Sun Quest out on the water and withdraw into himself more in the times between. Mrs. Brown was a wonderful help in keeping the Captain focused on things other than his declining health and increasing age.

The Browns and the Captain had become fast friends again after my bringing them together. And shortly afterward Mr. Brown had passed away. Since then the widow and widower were together several times each week. I was pleased for her attention to the Captain because my time had become busier than I had ever imagined it could be.

Late spring, summer and fall were our best times together, but even that was limited by my sports activities. Still we did manage to get together often enough to keep an eye on each other and keep up on the activities of one another during our many absences.

The lessons continued unabated, however. My Captain was squiring me to the submarine library, the Mystic docks to fuss over Sun Quest, and most often at his home to do the upkeep he couldn't manage any more. Mrs. Brown would be cleaning and I would be puttering on the deck or garage tool shed fixing one thing or another with the Captain hovering about reading me passages from books or asking me questions for an upcoming exam.

In this manner we passed a time of preparation for separation. And finally, inevitably the time came. I had graduated from high school and the summer had sped along with me continuing my nautical odd jobs. Then in August of '61 I made the move. I joined the US Navy with a promise of submarine school.

The ink was still wet on the papers when I arrived at my Captain's and prepared myself to tell him I was leaving in two weeks. "Captain, if you have a moment I would like to talk with you."

The Captain looked me in the eye and smiled. "You joined up, eh?"

"Yes, sir. I leave in two weeks for boot camp. Then back here for submarine school."

"Can't figure out why anyone would take a boat underwater on purpose." He smiled again. "Still, I can understand a man wanting to sail a while in his father's path."

"Thank you, Captain." An awkward silence, and then I continued. "I'll write often."

"I'll appreciate that li'l salt. I'll be counting on that, in fact." He pointed at me with his pipe stem. "Better make 'em good. I don't think the schoolmarm will let me keep them from her, and you know she won't be able to resist pointing out your dangling participles and other things dangling. If you get my drift."

I smiled nervously. "Yes, sir. I will be careful." Another awkward silence, and I again attempted to say what I really wanted to say. "Captain, I . . ." Tongue-tied I stopped and silence hung between us.

"Its OK lad, I know. Maybe we should go for a short sail, ya reckon?"

"That would be great Captain."

ENTERING NEW HARBORS

It was a perfect day for a sail on the Mystic River and beyond. And Sun Quest seemed to take care of herself so an old sea captain and the boy/man he had been mentoring for a decade found the path to say goodbye on their final cruise.

"You truly have Sun Quest fully rigged with all the latest technology, lad. Nicely done. And your attention to detail is impressive."

"Thank you Captain. I have had a great teacher."

"Teacher is only as good as his student, lad. And you have been as much the teacher here as I have been."

"Around the islands Captain?"

The Captain took a quick look to the skies and around the horizon before answering. "Aye lad. Good idea." A quick smile followed. "I don't want this to end either."

"Yes sir." I adjusted the sails for a tack around the farthest island. "Captain, I need to say this, so please help me by letting me get it all out, OK?"

"Aye, lad." And with the pipe routine telling me I had all the time I needed I began telling what mere words couldn't do justice and yet no other tools could come close.

"Captain I don't know what kind of life I will have, what I will do, or what I will become. And I know that is true for everyone. But I do know this. If it hadn't been for you and your patience, trust and confidence in me the path I would have traveled was destined to be short, painful and make no useful contribution."

I was facing the wind as I talked so I felt that the Captain couldn't tell that my tears were anything other than a reaction to the salt air in my eyes. I stood a little taller on the helm. "Oh Captain. My life will be a true blessing thanks to you and your investment in me." I looked into his eyes for the first time and realized that he had quite a bit of salt air in his also. "I wished hundreds of times that Neptune had made you my father. Then over the years I came to realize that in some very important ways it is much better that you are not my father by blood or adoption. Because by not being either of those and still doing all you have done for me your Love means all the more for it's voluntary nature."

"The great blessing to me that you are Captain; is that all the Love and respect you have given me was freely given. I will be eternally grateful Captain that you chose me. I know I can never deserve what you have given and continue to share. I also know I can invest my life and never repay you. I just want you to know that I get it. I honestly do understand how great a gift you're being in my life is. Even now, when all I can think to do is get away from my family, the hardest part is that to get away from them I must be away from you."

The Captain's pipe was out and he began to empty and refill it. "Thank you for the words, li'l salt. I'll remember them the rest of my life." A smile. "And I'll share them with Liddy for sure." He lit his pipe and took on a warm look as he continued. "You do understand this hasn't been a one way street, don't you?"

"Yes, sir. You have been very generous in making me feel like I contribute. But even though it isn't one way the two paths are like a forest path compared to a turnpike as far as giving."

"And the wonder of it is that your giving has been the turnpike of Love and respect, lad. While mine was the forest path of guidance." He seemed to have second thoughts and waved the pipe in a sweeping arch. "No, that isn't right." And he looked into my eyes. "You are so much more to me li'l salt. I Love you like a son. In fact I think my job is to Love you like a son for Liddy too. I am pained by your setbacks, and I nearly burst with pride at your achievements. And every day I measure success by how we have helped each other."

The Captain looked over the side of the boat into the water. "Now I also know why Liddy and I never had any children. This giving you up to your future is almost like dying, and I don't think we could have handled that in our lives. Tough enough to do it now at the end of my journey."

"Captain."

"No, please li'l salt, I let you have your say. Now it's my turn, ya reckon?"

"Yes, sir. I'm sorry. I just . . ."

"I know. I don't wish to be maudlin, just honest." He turned back to face me. "Lad, you have given me a decade of purpose to keep me alive. I was at the end of my rope." He paused and looked down at the water again. "Not unlike the ambassador."

He looked back up and directly into my eyes. "That day I first laid eyes on you. Somehow I knew that I would never be without a purpose again."

The Captain smiled in a manner that made his beard into a map of happiness for one last time. "By Neptune! You were such an urchin. You did need a lot of work."

"That's for sure."

"Oh, but lad when I looked into your eyes. Your eyes betrayed all the negatives your life gave you. There sparkling in those two little orbs was hope, love, happiness, thankfulness, and even a little pride. Oh those eyes told me I was embarking on an adventure." He leaned back and drew on the ivory pipe stem. "And an adventure it has been li'l salt. If I were to live another ten decades I wouldn't run out of stories."

We both knew somehow that this would be our final cruise, and the Captain set the tone for the rest of the way. "But just now lad. No stories. No more accolades. Lets just finish this sail together and be right here and now, ya reckon?"

"Aye, Captain." I looked out over the water in the direction I knew England resided. "The almanac indicates a harsh winter this year."

"Aye lad. And you'll be in boot camp in Chicago. Do you think you will have enough foul weather gear to handle it?"

"I guess so. The recruiter said that they issue all new gear when you arrive. And they take all your personal stuff and store it until graduation."

"You allowed to keep packages and such, if people mail them to you?"

"I don't know."

"You find out and let me know. If they do I'll send you some extra gear in the first week just to give you and edge."

"Thanks Captain." I smile a devilish smile. "That kind of warming up gear wouldn't include some medicinal brandy would it?"

"No li'l salt. That blasted navy's dry. They would only confiscate it. But we'll share one when you get here for school."

And the rest of the trip was invested in planning the future.

TYING ALONGSIDE

"I believe that was our best sail on Sun Quest li'l salt, ya reckon?"

"Aye Captain that it was."

"What should I do with her lad?"

"Sun Quest?"

"Aye."

"What do you want to do, Captain?"

"I want to keep her in shape for you to sail lad. But I don't think she will be sailed too often, ya reckon?"

"Not if she is counting on me Captain."

"So, lad, what should I do?"

I looked fondly at the sailboat I had spent so many wonderful hours on, then at my Captain. "I read once that a boat is secure when tied alongside in a harbor, but that wasn't where it was designed for. It is designed to sail out of the safe and secure area out onto the sea. So, for her sake I believe you should sell her to a good sailor, ya reckon?"

My Captain smiled and looked sad all at once. "Set her free to be all she can be. Just like I must do with you li'l salt. Just like I must do with you."

That salt air was simply filling our eyes with water. I walked the two steps between us and we fell into each other's arms. "I Love you Captain."

"And I Love you, son. I'll always Love you." He pulled himself back and looked me in the eyes. "My wish for you is that Neptune will always grant you steady winds and following seas. And may he grant that when you come to his kingdom and finish shaking his hand I may be next in line."

"If I have anything to say he may have a hard time being first."

"With the two of us, he just might step aside."

"Be here when I come back after my first trip at sea Captain. I will need to count on that. Then you're free."

"I'll be here for that, I promise."

DEBRIEFING

I did get to a submarine, and it was an old diesel sub like my dad had been on, so when I qualified to receive my Dolphins it was very special to me. In those days our great nation was changing over to new nuclear submarines and we didn't have too much to do in the way of helping in the cold war effort. So the navy in it's infinite wisdom sent some of us on public relations tours around the world.

I, at the ripe old age of 19 went on such a tour. Mind you it wasn't the same as sailing around the planet (I still haven't done that) but it was cruising the oceans in a complete circumnavigation, and that qualified as having gone round.

In our discourses by letter I kept the Captain up on what I saw going on in the world, and he gave me the American take on things. It was a tumultuous time actually. Ports like Hong Kong and Singapore taught sailors' one kind of lesson and the Middle East something else again.

We had left from San Diego and after nine months of the cruise having covered the Pacific and Indian Oceans, the Mediterranean Sea and the North Atlantic, we pulled into New London and I was able to take a few days leave to visit with my Captain.

"By Neptune if it weren't for the sailor suit I wouldn't have recognized you!"

"Nor I." Mrs. Brown was standing on the Captain's porch with him.

I now stood over six feet tall and still weighed the same as when I had graduated from high school, one hundred eighty five pounds. Only now I knew that my customized sharkskin sailors' suit was accenting my rippling muscles and I was proud enough that I had kept my pea coat off. "Well, Captain, I would sure recognize you. Even all formal dressed like you are."

"Paul, your English."

"Oh. Sorry ma'am. Can I make up for my poor English with a sailor's hug?"

"I thought you'd never ask. Come here you rapscallion." And I gave my best hug to that bear of a woman.

When we broke our grasp I said. "I've sailed the seven seas and never received a better hug, ma'am."

Mrs. Brown blushed and smiled. "Why thank you, Paul. That's very nice of you."

"By Neptune you've learned some lessons on your own, li'l salt. I've never possessed such a smooth tongue."

"Smooth tongue? No such thing Captain, just honesty, that's all."

"By Neptune, once around and your already qualified to sit at his court." He placed his hands on my shoulders. "Let me look at you lad." And he stepped back. "What a sight you are." He cocked his head toward the house conspiratorially. "I have that drink I promised you over a year ago."

"Great Captain. Just one though, as the ships diver I haven't been allowed to drink but two times this year."

"Two times. Must have been awful."

"Couldn't say. I remember the first beer and then they brought me back to the boat to sleep it off."

"Well, faith in me timbers, we can't stand out here all day. Lets get on with that drink."

"Aye, aye, sir."

We enjoyed a wonderful afternoon together, and Mrs. Brown fixed a great dinner. The Captain had arranged with the new owner of Sun Quest that I could take her out for a few hours shake down cruise, which I thoroughly enjoyed. Mrs. Brown asked that I visit her at her home and I did so on the second day.

"Thank you for coming, Paul. I have fixed some tea and cookies."

"Thank you, ma'am. You seemed to have something you wanted to talk about. It is important?"

"Yes, I wanted you to hear it from me before you leave so you and the Captain can say your goodbyes." She drew in a deep breath and continued. "The Captain has a terminal illness and will not be with us for much longer."

"Yes, ma'am. I know that."

"Oh, of course, he told you."

"No, ma'am. No one told me. I have just known for a long while now that the Captain wouldn't be able to hold on much longer. We both know this is our last time together."

"Oh. I see. I'm sorry I wasted your time."

"Ma'am you haven't wasted my time. I wanted to talk with you also."

"What is it, Paul."

"I wanted to thank you for being so very strong for the Captain, ma'am." I took her hand in mine. "The Captain wouldn't tell you, but you are in every letter he has sent me. He marvels at your strength and is very grateful for your help and support during these difficult times for him. His pain is something awful, I guess."

"He tries not to let on, but it is often very obvious that he is in pain."

"Ma'am, my submarine is leaving in two days and I must be on it. We still have to go around South America and I won't be back in San Diego for three more months. My hope is he will hold on and I can have one more visit, but I believe that he will be gone before then."

"Why is that?"

"He promised me he would hold on till I returned from my first trip at sea, and so far I haven't convinced him that meant me returning to my homeport in San Diego and not returning to him." I looked down at the coffee table that probably never saw a cup of coffee. "I didn't know we would visit here, I probably should have known a submarine, even a Pacific one, would pull into New London, but I just didn't think it through. Anyway, I think after I leave he will get himself ready to go to Liddy. And Neptune!" I hastily added.

"All I want to ask is that you be with him to the end. Would you do that?"

"Of course, Paul. But lets not be defeatist. Perhaps we can keep him around till your return."

"Yes, ma'am. Thank You." I rose. "Ma'am if there is nothing else I need to spend time with the Captain."

"Of course." She looked at me seriously. "Your family?"

"They don't know I'm here. And I would like to keep it that way. Just too little time for all that stuff."

"I understand." I reached for my hat. "Paul."

"Yes ma'am."

"Please take care of yourself. It's a dangerous world out there."

"Don't worry ma'am. Neptune doesn't want any part of me just yet."

"Good. I'll see you when you return in three months?"

"Yes ma'am, you can count on it."

"Thank you." She paused and placed a hand on my cheek. "For everything."

"And you ma'am." We hugged and I left.

"Well, li'l salt looks like our time together is coming to an end, ya reckon?"

"Yes sir looks that way." I smiled. "It was wonderful Captain. Thanks."

"For me as well li'l salt. For me as well." He paused on our way to the porch. "You keep on writing will you? I get a kick out of your stories. That barrier reef diving you told of in Australia must have been really something."

"Yes sir it truly was something special."

We came to the porch and turned and the Captain reached out his hand, which I took, placed at my side and took him into my arms. "I Love you Captain. I hope you are here for my return."

"I Love you too, son." He paused and withdrew from our hug enough to look into my eyes. "I can't wait to tell Liddy all about our adventures. She'll adore you."

I knew I was looking at my Captain for the last time. I drew back, stood at attention and rendered my very best salute. The Captain drew himself together and returned the salute. We smiled at each other and I walked down the stairs and away from the best friend I have ever had.

CHAPTER SEVEN

VOYAGING AND LIVING

LETTERS FROM THE HEREAFTER

Upon returning to San Diego I, along with the rest of the crew, were given our last month's mail. In my case it would be the last thing I would receive from my Captain. The envelope was very thick and the return address was Mrs. Brown's Farm. She had a short cover letter from her, and one she had written for the Captain the last week of his life. I walked out on the fantail of the submarine and sat down to read the letters.

First her letter:

> My Dearest Paul,
>
> I hope this finds you well and happy. I just completed the last project with your friend and mentor Captain Armbruster yesterday, and found out early this morning that he passed on during the early morning hours today. I have thanked you many times for bringing me together with that fine man, and for helping me heal from the loss of his wife, my best friend ever. But now I feel a pain of loss which I never would have imagined possible for that old seafarer.
>
> I think you already know that the Captain has, over the years, come to believe that God (who he still referred to

as *Neptune*) *gave you to him to provide the final fulfillment of his mission in life. And, I believe, to be the son he never had.*

His letter to you is wonderful, so I won't interfere with your reading of it, except to say that this last week with him while doing this letter was one of my most rewarding exercises. You will be pleased to note that I have withheld the English Teacher's hand and simply acted as the Captain's scribe. With all of its errors I have never read a more significant work of Love. I was very grateful to the Captain that he allowed me to work with him during his last week of life on earth to create the attached letter to you. Both you and the Captain have taught me that the form of the words isn't as important as the feelings behind them.

The Captain was very weak, and our sessions were three or four times each day for a few minutes each while he dictated his final thoughts to you, and perhaps to the rest of the world someday.

When you return to Mystic, please make time for a visit to the farm. I would really like that. I took the liberty of making several copies and the Captain graciously signed them all for you, they will be here when you come home, along with his sextant.

No matter what I ever said as your teacher those three years, I want you to know that I now realize that your youthful enthusiasms have touched the lives of so many here in such wonderful ways that you will never be forgotten. May God bless you and give you a good life.

Faithfully Yours,
Mrs. Helen Brown

And now the Captain's:

CAPTAIN JOSIAH T. ARMBRUSTER

Dear Li'l' Salt,

The school Marm is helping me with this missive. I owe her a lot for her help over these last few months of being bedridden. Of course, it is just one more thing that I owe you for. Without your intervention we would never have made peace with out pasts and enjoyed such a great friendship these last few years. Thank you, Lil salt, for that and so much more.

By the time you read this I will be with Neptune, that's the deal I made with the schoolmarm. After I die she mails it to you on that submarine of yours. Probably heading back to America by then.

Now, don't you fret, we've talked about this on many occasions, and we agreed that it is the normal course of events. So, no sadness now, I'll tolerate none of that. I led a full life before the mast. I was privileged to have a wonderful woman Love me and be my partner for life. I have enjoyed friendships and family; pain and pleasure, highs and lows. What a journey! I remember your description of the barrier reef off Australia, and I am pleased that I chose the seaward side of my life's reef. I know that you will do so as well.

And you also convinced me that Neptune's Son, Jesus, will make sure that Liddy is with me. I am also grateful that it will be a long time before you sail your last cruise and join us. The ways you touch people and bring out their best needs to be around for a long time.

You're free from abuse now lad and that gives me a measure of peace. I only wish I could free your mind of the emotional sea bag he dumped on you. You will have to fight that battle the rest of your life. And a great life it will be. And that gives me a measure of satisfaction and pleasure.

Lil Salt, I want to thank you for adding life to these, old sea dogs, last years and doing it in a way that makes for wonderful memories and mental pictures. Neptune blessed me when he brought you into my life. Liddy and I never had any children, and that's all right, it was God's plan that we focus on each other. This last decade watching you grow into a man filled a void I didn't even know I had. And I know Liddy was there with us to enjoy every minute. You helped me relearn what it is to Love.

I know that I have been the one who is the recognized teacher in our time together, but I was only teaching skills for leading a productive life. You were teaching me how to live a full one. And I will be forever grateful Lil' Salt. (End of day one)

I am looking over the cove and out to the Sound. In the next few days I'll be seeing Neptune come for me. I hate being in bed, and these confound nurses are more trouble than a steward at sea. I do admit that your blamed schoolmarm is a delight though. The stories we have shared about my treasured Liddy have made the last year go by rapidly and pleasantly. Her husband was a lucky man.

Lil' Salt, I want so much to make this a reminder of all the lessons we have shared, and the pure wonder I have enjoyed this last decade watching you become a man. Unfortunately all I can remember is what I have learned from you. Your trusting nature. Your enthusiasm and vigor in everything you do, and every day you live. I hope you never lose those particular parts of your nature. Indeed, if they haven't been beaten out of you by now, most probably they'll be there throughout your life. And those who know you will be the beneficiaries.

I know my life was not only extended, but also made fuller for the time I was with you and the projects we completed together. (End of day two)

Tough night. I'll have to work faster if I am to finish this before I get with Neptune. Hope the schoolmarm can keep up. Now, listen up. You need to remember the lessons we lived.

First, make sure that what you are doing is what you want to be doing, and that it is the right thing to be doing. I know you chose submarines because of your dad's being lost in the war, and I know you will be good at anything you do, but I also know that you will move on to other adventures in your life. When you do, make sure to take the time to think it through. And when you decide, don't second-guess or look back. Give it everything you've got. Everything!

I know you know this, but it is too important to go unsaid just now. Next, never stop practicing your skills, and always work at improving your mind. Keep on reading and writing, and most important thinking. Remember that old adage that 2% of a people think, 3% think they think, and 95% would rather die than think! Make damn sure you are always in the 2%. (End of day three)

Remember Lil' salt, as much as possible, keep worries from your life. It is only destructive, never helpful or positive. Plan, work the plan, and enjoy the ride. But never worry.

I'll never forget the first time you left the cove and sailed into the river and on to Noank in that little rowboat we made into a fair to middelen sailboat. I also remember watching you in that Nor'Easter. When I lost sight of you that time I thought I had lost you forever. But I never remember seeing fear in your eyes through my telescope, just determination, and even a hint of a smile. You are some kind of a sailor, lad.

Well, like I was sayin'. No worry, and don't ever fear the first step after your planning is complete. Get out of the safe harbors of life, and live to the fullest.

Then, when you have lived fully, and your time here is short, give back. I know your generous spirit will make that the easy part. My estate settlement is going the way we discussed. I remember your refusal to accept anything but the sextant. Everything will be sold and the funds go for maritime scholarships you think are so great. (End of day four)

I have to end this now. I saw Neptune last night, and he left me today to get this done. So, I'll clear the harbor and fill the sails for you lad.

Thank you for allowing me into your life. It has been a great way to round out my time here. You have given me much more than you'll ever know or believe. But some day I hope you can understand it when the person you mentor gives you more than you give him. Funny, how at the end we don't think of all the successes in life, just the people in it. Thanks to you my last years have been healing ones. I even came to care deeply about the schoolmarm here, who is writing this for me, thanks to your chicanery. Yes, I knew you tricked us both into getting together. And I'll be eternally grateful.

I was in my thirties before I had sailed in all seven seas, and you will have done it before your twentieth birthday. Just one more indication of just how much you'll do in your life. Blast Neptune for taking me! Damnation I want to see your smiling face just once more. The picture of you with the beard! That was something! Getting too tired to think straight. Of course I know that as soon as I join Neptune he'll let me see your face again. And you won't know when so you better keep that smile on it, just in case.

There is so much to say, but I don't have the energy now. Besides we did say most things when we were together. Only one thing more to say. I Love you, Son. I have since the first time I laid eyes on you on that rock. You're a beautiful child of Neptune lad. Now, take my Love, respect and admiration with you as you begin your voyage of sailing through life.

Your Captain and friend,

Scribbled in his frail hand after the signature was his final
wish . . .

May Neptune give you smooth winds and following seas.

YOUR NEXT JOURNEYS

The promontory over Mystic harbor, which was comprised
of the cemetery where my captain was laid to rest, was incredible
in its visage. The sky was on the verge of becoming a storm, yet
was clear enough that the sun was warming the grass and me
between clouds. The wind was blowing the flap on the back of
my uniform up onto the back of my head, and as I looked over
the harbor and the sights of my youth I felt a peace I had not
known since the last time I had been with my captain.

"Well, Captain you sure picked a great place to spend eternity."
Then I looked up into the heavens, and back down to his grave.
"I know that it is only your physical shell left in that hole,
Captain." Then I looked back to the heavens. "But your spirit
will probably use this location to sit with Liddy and share our
stories." A smile crosses my face. "And I'll bet Neptune will be
listening. You are such a great storyteller that he won't be able to
resist."

"I asked Mrs. Brown, the schoolmarm, to wait in the car so
I could be alone with you Captain. We are going to go to dinner
at the Stonington yacht club. She wants to see the plaque and
hear about the last great sail of Endeavor." Another conspiratorial
smile crosses my face. "Yes, captain, I kinda want to know if I
have become a legend at the club, or just another footnote to
local sailing lore. I'm willing to bet on the latter."

I look around the cemetery and the view beyond.
"Captain . . . I miss you, sir. I find myself really glad when I have
lots of work to do because I don't dwell on your being gone. I
ache inside when I think of living on without your being available
to me." I kick the ground. "I went to your home today. The new
owners are nice people and let me walk out on the deck. But

they are landlubbers Captain. A sorry state of affairs when such a wonderful Captain's home is occupied by landlubbers." A look to the heavens and another smile moves my lips and brightens my eyes. "Could be worse. At least they're not from New York." The smile diminishes and I remove my white hat. "Oh captain. Why is it that we go on without the ones we love?"

Suddenly the wind did a complete 180' turn and was coming directly into my face. As the wind blew over me I felt as if it were caressing me carefully and I could feel as much as hear my Captain. "Li'l Salt, we have brought out the best in each other. You go on without me to take us to those who need our help. Show them a full life. And tell them how it is so readily available to them also."

"Give a full measure to everything you do lad. Stay on a right and true course throughout your voyage. Lead by example. But lead you must. The transfer of truths from one generation to another must be coupled with the benefit of the latter one's experiences to be made all the more valuable for those who follow."

"Lad, you are to build on the foundation we laid together. That foundation of caring and mutual respect grew to Love for us. Now you go forward and share with others that the way for us to reach our potential is Love."

"Lad, just as you can now feel this Love with Neptune's Wind, you must take it on to the future. Our spirits are with you on your journey. Just as yours will help others when you join us."

"Now go lad. Take Mrs. Brown to dinner at the yacht club. And li'l salt, I'll just take that bet on your legendary status."

The wind slowly abated and then returned to it's previous heading, again slapping my uniform flap on the back of my head. I looked out over the harbor and the sky and finally down at the gravesite of my Captain. I replaced my hat on my head, stood at attention, and snapped a salute. "Aye, aye Captain!" And with that I began the walk back to the car with Mrs. Brown in it. And as I continued on and realized what had just happened I rose to my full height, my steps became more purposeful, and a smile crossed my lips as I felt a surge of confidence pass through me. I was headed on to my future, and thanks to my captain I was well prepared.

Another crooked smile at the heavens coupled with a wink. "Thanks Captain."